Horses
and
Other Voices

Enjoy!

Letitia Sanders

Horses
and
Other Voices

Letitia Sanders

HUNTLEIGH PRESS
NOVATO, CALIFORNIA

Huntleigh Press
www.huntleighpress.com

Cover art, serigraph "Pasture" by Mike Smith
Photos:
Karen Andersen page 6
Clare Long page 58
Karen Sheets pages: opposite Preface, 80, 136
Sheri Scott pages: 16, 110

Horses and Other Voices/Letitia Sanders—1st ed.
ISBN 978-0-9961489-0-0
Library of Congress Number: 2015903812

Printed in the United States of America

I dedicate this book to D.J., Rommel, Shamina, Riff, Merlin, Jamaica, Obadiah, Tuptim and Angus whom I hope to see again someday.

For Angus MacNabb

About the Book

Many of the people, animals, and events in this book are based on real ones. However, I have taken much liberty to make them more interesting, more colorful or more sympathetic. I have exaggerated situations, and in a few places I have changed very sad endings into happy ones as I feel that is the advantage of Art over Reality. Even the narrator is an idealized version of myself with insights and abilities I wish I had.

Acknowledgements

Many of my friends read early versions of this book to test my explanations of horse related terms, especially the discipline of dressage and breeds. I would like to thank them for their time and patience—Karen Andersen, Pat Arrigoni, Rachel Downing, Carole Gray, Jean James, Maria Norall, Genna Panzarella, and Nansi Timmer. Penn Fullerton encouraged me to turn my short stories into a book, and Marion Wiener whipped them into shape. Patti Schofler contributed much from her experience in the showing and judging of dressage.

Many professionals in the book publishing industry were also involved. Thanks to Book Passage's Path to Publishing program and Sam Barry for putting me in touch with Linda Jo Meyer and Jim Shubin, a most talented and creative book designer.

I could not have put the pieces of the puzzle together without BAIPA, Bay Area Independent Publishers Association, and their monthly Saturday meetings, bagels and all. They put me into contact with Ruth Schwartz, The Wonderlady and her Complete Book Midwife Program, who never lost her patience throughout the process.

I am excited that the well-known artist Mike Smith allowed me to use his serigraph, "Pasture" for the cover.

I especially appreciate the patience of my husband, Donn Downing, whose experience as a correspondent for *Time* magazine made him very sympathetic to my midnight doubts.

Table of Contents

Preface   1

Shaman   7

Salem—La Belleza Negra   17

The Ranch   33

Mama Kitty   39

Buster   49

Foster   59

Lipizzaner Ladies   69

Scout   81

Mocha   93

Chief   101

Pablo   111

Wanda   121

Cincinnati   131

Jason   137

Smokey   145

Dr. Stern   155

Epilogue: Twenty Years Later   165

Online Glossary   171

₩

Preface

Do animals go to heaven?

That was the question I wrote on a piece of paper and submitted to our preacher at his yearly question and answer session at the Sunday night service. It was 1950 and I was a little girl, ten years old.

"No," he answered as he crumpled the sheet and dropped it on the floor by the pulpit. "Because they don't have souls."

I knew he was wrong then, and I am more sure now. At the Ranch I saw many times how the soul of an animal joined with the soul of a person to bring both them and me closer to whatever heaven may exist.

I don't pretend that I planned it that way. It just happened. It was serendipity. I had selected the Ranch as the place to take my own young horse to be trained when I realized that I wasn't capable of doing the job myself. I was 53 years old and had worked my whole life. I had just retired from my job at a major computer company. I was bored from not having enough to do at home. So I volunteered to work on weekends in the Ranch's office, answering the phones or being available to call 911 in case of emergency.

Eventually this evolved into my working four days a week as assistant Barn Manager. I oversaw the two

Mexican workers and was generally responsible for the smooth running of the facility when the owner wasn't there. The fact that I was studying Spanish at the local community college was probably one of my best qualifications for the job, in spite of the fact that "manure" was not standard vocabulary at school.

I had picked the Ranch because of its facilities and its distance of only thirty minutes from my house. It had one indoor and three outdoor rings. There were two trainers who were highly qualified to train young horses. I must admit that I personally was swayed by the Coke machine and the nice indoor toilet.

My going to work at the Ranch was really a trip back to an earlier self. From the time I was little girl, I had always been close to animals. My cats and horses were my escape from the pressures of family and a demanding social life. When fear of an algebra test or of not having a date for the Saturday dance made me nervous, I would curl up somewhere with a furry friend or go hang out at my pony's stable. Somehow those warm bodies calmed and restored me to my strongest self. The animals accepted me and reassured me that everything would be fine.

I don't think that is abnormal. People and animals have been interdependent for centuries. It is only in the last one hundred years that we humans have relied on machines for our happiness and support.

My first experience with owning a horse was when I was in the second grade. I had probably learned to love horses from going to the movies on Saturday mornings. The famous horses, Trigger and Champion, were as big film stars as their owners, Roy Rogers and Gene Autry.

Also every afternoon at five there was the whinny of the Lone Ranger's horse, Silver, on the radio.

So when I saw a preview of *The Red Pony* by Steinbeck at the movie theatre, the thing I wanted most in the world was for my father to go to the movie with me. I knew my father also loved horses, and I wanted to share my passion with him. He agreed to go on the evening of the last day of the show.

My father was a very busy, hard-working trial lawyer in our small town. When Thursday came, he truly wasn't able to get home in time to make it to the movie. When he did come home, he found me crying on my bed. I am not sure I have ever been as disappointed since.

He went to the telephone and called a number. I heard him ask several questions, and then he returned to my room.

"Get dressed," he said. "We're going somewhere."

It was very dark outside the windows of the car. Soon there were no lights from the streets of the town. We drove far into the country and finally stopped at a huge barn with a windmill pump in front. I recognized it as belonging to Mr. Keith who bought and sold mostly mules, but also some horses.

I got out of the car and followed Daddy into the dim interior with its wonderful smell of hay, warm bodies and manure. Mr. Keith in his baggy overalls led us to a stall. At first I thought it was empty because, unlike all the others, there was no large equine head above the wooden walls.

Daddy held me up to look inside. Down below I saw what looked at first like one of the black and white hide rugs that was always on the floor of the movie ranch houses. Then it moved and turned into a fat pinto pony.

"Will she do?" Daddy asked.

"Oh, yes," I answered. "What is its name?"

"Whatever you want it to be," Daddy responded with a smile.

"I think I'll call it Paint," was my uninspired answer.

"You'll mean you'll call her Paint," Daddy said. "You must always refer to a horse by its correct sex. Paint is a mare, a lady horse."

Then Daddy reached into his pocket and pulled out his wallet. "How much do I owe you, Mr. Keith?"

So Paint, the pony, came to live in our backyard. Daddy partitioned off half of the garage for her stall. She made much more work for him. Every day when he came home from the courthouse, he would clean out her stall and put more hay in her feed trough. I feel guilty about it now. I didn't help very much, but I think Daddy enjoyed it as an escape from the tension of his work. I feel that way now when I occasionally clean out my Shaman's stall instead of waiting for the workers at the Ranch to do the job.

Soon a large manure pile began to grow behind the garage. It nourished Mother's roses and provided worms for fishing. I must admit that I really didn't ride Paint very much as our house was in the middle of town, and I had to wait for Daddy to go with me to get out into the country.

We thought it was hilarious when Paint would answer back to the call from The Lone Ranger's horse, Silver, on the radio in the kitchen. I learned to produce a very acceptable whinny myself which was appreciated later at college parties. Now I wonder what Silver and I were actually saying.

But Paint was a good friend. I spent many summer mornings with her out in the field behind our house. From Paint I learned how therapeutic brushing a horse could be.

But that was a long time ago, and both Paint and Daddy are gone. When I came to the Ranch, I was well over half a century old, retired, and looking for a new life. I was going to find it at a horse ranch in northern California.

Shaman

The Ranch was not Shaman's first home.

He was born on a hill overlooking a remote bay of the Pacific Ocean. During the day he stood in the warm gold sunlight. At night he watched the fog slowly creep over the low hills hiding the inlet below, turning his whole world blue-gray. Around him grazed five other members of the small herd of Arabians, those deceptively delicate seeming creatures who are among the toughest horses in the world.

I first saw the little bay colt when he was two days old. The white blaze on his nose looked almost too large. His three white stockings made his long legs look even more delicate than normal.

He was his mother's first baby. She didn't understand when he pushed his nose under her belly, trying to nurse. She would just turn her head to look at him and move away. My friend, her owner, asked me to hold his mother still while she helped Shaman get his breakfast. It didn't take long before they both caught on.

That may have been when Shaman first decided that he wanted to be my horse. At the time I was working in the city all week and coming to the farm on the coast on weekends to ride Sheriff, one of the other members of the herd. My friend on Shaman's mother and I would spend hours riding over the hilly trails of the parklands surrounding Shaman's home.

Whenever I went into the pasture with halter in hand to catch up Sheriff, Shaman would meet me at the gate. He would walk up to me and stand perfectly still, as if afraid that even the slightest move might frighten me off. His big eyes searched my face, and his lovely, curved and pointed ears followed my every move. After accepting his pat, he would follow me wherever I went.

Shaman had decided he was my horse.

At the time, I had no intention of owning a horse. I had a perfect setup with free access to the smooth-riding, well-trained, obedient Sheriff. The only cost to me was his monthly feed bill of about $30. I lived in a small condominium in the city and had no place, not even a tent, to keep a horse.

But Shaman had a different agenda. Slowly, something happened to me that had happened only a couple of times before. I recognized that I had fallen in love, not with a man this time, but with the now gangly two-year-old colt registered as Soaring Eagle's Shaman.

So I followed my heart and bought Shaman.

Shaman's schooling began at three months when he learned to wear a halter and follow the person holding the lead rope. He knew that the word "whoa" meant to stop and that the word "walk" meant to move forward slowly. He even learned to ride in the horse trailer, although at his first loading he was so little that he backed out under the butt chain that hits most horses at the knees.

When Shaman was two years old, my friend Katherine, who had done much of the training of Shaman's mother, began to put him on a longe line and teach him to walk and trot around and around in circles. He learned "trot" in both directions and to pay close attention to what was being asked of him. At three years he even learned to wear a saddle and bridle.

The first time I climbed up on his back, he spread his feet to adjust to my weight and looked back at me with a puzzled look. He liked to please and was very quick to learn.

The problem was that my friend and I weren't professional trainers and could only safely go so far with his training. That was when Shaman moved to the Ranch.

Shaman did not share my approval of the place at first. He had never had a roof over his head, and it took us an entire hour to coax him into the barn. He wasn't bad; he just refused to move. He would not be tempted by food or kind words. Finally he had his beautiful behind tapped lightly by a whip, something that had never happened to him before. He just turned to look at it.

When he finally was coaxed into a stall, he paced around nervously, obviously unhappy with his confinement. He let go of his fears by forming an immediate deep attachment to his neighbor, a huge chestnut jumper named Sydney.

Shaman's formal training had begun. At first anyone could see that, like a young boy sent off to boarding school for the first time, he was homesick. He missed his pasture, his ocean inlet and the fog covered hills. He grieved for his herd and his freedom.

When I bought Shaman, I had intended that he would be a trail horse like his mother. I would only leave him in training at the Ranch for a few months. Then I would take him back to the coast to ride the trails with his mother and Sheriff.

But things turned out differently. His training with Harriett, the hunter/jumper trainer, started well enough, but it soon became evident that his real talent lay in his wonderful floating trot and precise movements. He did not have the aggressiveness a jumper needs to charge around over fences. Worst of all, he really didn't like to canter, which is the main gait used in jumping.

It became clear to me that Shaman was more like Mikhail Baryshnikov, the dancer, than Joe Montana, the football player—both graceful athletes, but with very different temperaments. Shaman would never become a good jumper. Besides at fifty years old, I was too old to jump horses.

I decided Shaman really wanted to become a dressage horse, one of the ballet dancers of the horse world.

Arabian horses like Shaman were first brought to this country in 1598 when Juan de Onate brought about 350 Spanish Arabian horses from Mexico and settled them near what is now Santa Fe, New Mexico. About a century later, most of them had been acquired by the Native Americans, and 200 years later in 1806, Lewis and Clark encountered them on the upper reaches of the Missouri River on their expedition to the Pacific Ocean.

Arabian horses were reintroduced into the U.S. in the first decade of the 20th century. Many breeders emphasized their beauty and spirit over their intelligence and stamina. They were bred for looks only and encouraged to exhibit explosive behavior. But by the middle of the century, many riders began to appreciate the good sense and surefootedness of the original imports. They were prized as great for trail riding, and the old bloodlines became popular again.

The problem for Shaman and me was that now few people believed an Arabian horse could become a dressage horse. That discipline had for centuries been the domain of the European-bred horses: the Hanoverians, the Andalusians, and most famous of all, the white Lipizzaners of Vienna. These horses had set the style of the large, stocky, controlled dressage horse. A small Arabian would be too quick and flighty and would look out of place in the world of dressage. It just hadn't been done.

But Shaman and I were lucky. The dressage trainer at the Ranch was a very pretty, petite 25-year-old with long blonde hair named Heidi. She had ridden Arabians early in her career and noticed Shaman as I was leading him around in his first days at the Ranch.

"Is he a 'Khemosabi' baby?" she asked. "He resembles that famous Arabian stallion."

She was not surprised when I told her that Khemosabi was his grandfather. She looked at Shaman closely and gave him a trainer's highest compliment, "He's nice!"

Two things finally propelled Shaman toward dressage: the sheep and the back turnout. The ring where Harriett worked Shaman was the Oak Tree arena at the far back end of the Ranch. Whoever owned the land next to it brought in four sheep. From someplace in his desert genes or for some other more immediate reason, Shaman was afraid of these creatures.

Since Shaman had never been a nervous horse, neither Harriett nor I realized how afraid he was until one day when she left him in the back turnout area, farthest away from the other horses and closest to the sheep. He was terrified. He called and cried out and ran until he was coated in white, foamy sweat.

From that day on he never worked well in this arena or with Harriett. He was too afraid. The Arabian horse's quality of learning very fast and never forgetting had been awakened—and would probably take years to change.

So Shaman left Harriet and went to train with Heidi. They were a perfect combination. Her very gentle, quiet methods were perfect for Shaman. Her worst punishment was a loud "No!" and she often addressed him as "Mr. Shaman."

Yet anyone who thought Heidi was soft was wrong. She demanded absolute perfection from her students, both horse and human. Shaman understood this and agreed completely. He was able to be perfect, and he wanted to show me, Heidi, and everyone else that he could be. He had inherited the Arabian horse's capacity for discipline and close bonds with people. He thrived on the hard work and control of dressage training.

As the next year went by, I forgot about my goal of having Shaman be my trail horse. I rode less and less and watched more and more as Heidi took Shaman through the different figures and movements of dressage. All my years of casual trail riding had not prepared me for the precision of dressage and my fifty-year-old body rebelled. But even more, I preferred to watch the magic that happened between Heidi and Mr. Shaman. It was like choosing to go to watch the ballet over dancing the two-step with a friend.

I discovered something else about Shaman when I entered and rode him in two small amateur schooling shows at the Ranch. I had wanted to see if I had the nerve and also how Shaman would behave with all the people and confusion. What I discovered should not have surprised me given Shaman's famous grandfather, Khemosabi.

I found out that Shaman was a ham. Instead of being frightened by the audience, he loved it. Instead of being spooked by the applause, he courted it.

He was on his best behavior and seemed to feel that the entire small show was being put on for his own benefit. In spite of my rather poor riding, we found ourselves in second place. Shaman loved the audience and the audience loved him. The judge told me afterwards that Shaman was the cutest horse she had ever seen.

It wasn't long before the next step seemed inevitable; Heidi instead of me should show Shaman. We decided to enter him in the dressage events of the local Arabian horse club's upcoming show.

Heidi worked hard teaching Shaman the First Level Test 1 in the official national dressage handbook. With its exact turns and figures, the test is not unlike a ballet company's choreography for a traditional ballet like *Swan Lake*. It had to be perfect for Heidi.

Shaman agreed. Every hoof had to be in the right place at the right speed as they did twenty meter circles at each end of the arena and changed gaits from trot to canter and back again at the precise spots marked by the numbers along the sides of the dressage court. Finally Heidi was satisfied with their progress.

The next step was to make Shaman as beautiful as he could be. The day before the show, I bathed him, taking care that his white socks looked as though they had just come back from a French laundry. We washed and combed his thick black tail and trimmed it straight across in the international dressage bang cut.

His mahogany coat shone in the sun as we covered it with his blanket so he would stay clean overnight. I was at the Ranch at 6:00 AM on the morning of the show to put his mane in the short doubled-over braids the dressage rules require. Even a long, thick, black Arabian mane must show discipline in a dressage show.

All around the Ranch were horse trailers surrounded by huge horses. There were Swedish and Dutch Warmbloods, Hanoverians, Thoroughbreds, and even an Oldenburg or two. As Heidi led Shaman quietly toward the show arena, he looked very small and insignificant compared to the other entries. He shyly looked around with his head rather low and his tail nervously clamped flat against his behind.

I could see that he was a little afraid and insecure, and I wished I had not entered him in this show. I was afraid he would shy badly at the decorative pots of flowers placed around the rails of the dressage court.

At our small schooling shows we had not had music. How would Shaman react to the loud strains of Mozart in the air? What would he make of the bright yellow umbrella shading the judges' stand?

When Shaman's name was finally called, Heidi rode him into the arena. Shaman didn't like the pots of white chrysanthemums at the entrance, but he gritted his teeth and went past them anyway. During the one minute of warm-up time before the actual test, Shaman seemed a little distracted by the people lining the rails. They went past the judges' stand, and Shaman gave a little buck.

Then he settled down to business. As he trotted by me, I could see in his eyes that he had decided to do his best.

From then on it was perfection—not a wrong move, not a second's delay. He was Baryshnikov on the stage, an artist.

It became very quiet as the little horse floated around the court. His thick, black tail was lifted high and moved in perfect balance to his turns. His white feet moved so quickly and evenly that he seemed to be a mechanical toy horse. His beautiful head was very still and soft on the arch of his neck. At the final halt and salute to the judge, the little horse stood square and quiet as a statue in the middle of the loud applause.

Shaman had done it. He had earned a score of 71.68 percent, highest score of the whole show. The smallest horse had received the biggest score of all. Of course, he was only at First Level now, but he proved he could do the same through the other levels and all the way to Grand Prix level with time and work.

Salem-La Belleza Negra

The black mare in the crossties grooming area was one of the most striking horses I had ever seen. But when I approached her perfectly formed head, she turned toward me with her ears laid back threateningly.

Her coat was a shiny black that reminded me of a crow's wing. Her legs were slim and delicate. Her thick black tail, which was cut straight across at the bottom in the international dressage style, was so long that it almost touched the ground. There was not a speck of white on her.

"She is lovely," I said to her owner, an attractive older woman in slim riding pants, who had just finished saddling her. "What is her name?"

"Salem," she said as she mounted and rode toward the dressage court.

Heidi was standing beside me watching their departure from her crosstie area. "That's one of my new trainees," she said. "That horse won international Western Pleasure Champion at age three. She is eight now and has been winning consistently for the last five years."

I was not too impressed. In my opinion Western Pleasure was the class in a show that required the least training and skill on the part of both horse and rider. Almost any horse that could perform the basic gaits of walk, trot and canter could qualify as a Western Pleasure horse.

Horses usually won this class on looks, rather than performance. Fancy western costumes for the rider and silver encrusted saddles for the horses seemed to take the prize. As a devotee of dressage, which required years of training, I was a little snobbish on the subject. I was probably wrong.

There are many breeds of horses all over the world and many books filled with pictures and descriptions of them. There is an oversimplified way to look at them. The vastly different types of horses have been divided into three categories, the cold bloods, the warm bloods, and the hot bloods.

The cold bloods and the hot bloods are at the extremes with the warm bloods in the middle. The cold bloods are the large, slower draft horses like the Budweiser horses, the Clydesdales. Originally these were primarily workhorses that were used to pull plows and wagons.

The hot bloods are the Arabians and Thoroughbreds prized for speed and agility. Arabians are the purest of the modern breeds due to their history of isolation in the desert. Their small size makes them quick and maneuverable. Thoroughbreds were developed from breeding Arabian stallions to large cold-blooded mares in the eighteenth century to make them faster on the racetrack. In fact, all Thoroughbreds must trace their lineage back to one of three Arabian stallions. Although they were originally bred to race, they are now used for other purposes, even trail riding.

The warm bloods are also a combination of the solid working cold bloods and the hotter Arabians. They were used mostly as warhorses in Europe centuries ago, and there are many different varieties or breeds. The high level of training and physical ability necessary to make them controllable for combat and parades eventually became the discipline of dressage that we know today. What began as military maneuvers became the art we now see at the Olympics. The military uniforms gave way to the top hats and tailcoats of the dressage riders. The tall shiny black boots remained from the battlefields and parade ground. The best know breeds of warm bloods are the Hanoverians from Germany, the Lipizzaners from Austria, and the Andalusians from Spain, but there are many others. It takes years of training to become a high level dressage horse.

I was surprised that at this point Salem's owner, whose name was Theodora, was shifting over to dressage from a field where they had been so successful. There seemed to be something mysterious about it.

"She certainly is a beauty," I answered trying to avoid the cattiness that can so often be a part of the horse world, "What breed is she?"

"A Morgan," Heidi replied.

"That's funny," I said. "She doesn't look like a Morgan to me. She reminds me of the Tennessee Walking Horses my father used to raise. She looks like the famous old stallion, Midnight Sun."

"That's nuts," Heidi returned. "To me she looks more like the American Saddlebred breed."

"Oh well," I answered. "They are all American breeds that come from rather mixed bloodlines and probably even have some of the same early ancestors together. That would explain it."

I watched as the horse and her owner went around the dressage court. The horse was certainly a fast mover and looked wonderful under saddle. The men who worked at the Ranch often had their own names for the horses. They called Salem "La Belleza Negra" or Black Beauty in Spanish.

As the spring weeks passed, Salem's dressage training progressed rapidly. She already had the basics down, so all Heidi had to do was to teach the horse and her owner the niceties of dressage. Theodora learned how to put the horse in what is called a collected frame. This makes it look like the horse that is the chessboard piece, with its neck curved, instead of like a racehorse with its neck stretched out for the finish line.

Then Salem began to learn the figures of dressage that make the sport not unlike competition ballroom dancing or ice skating. The twenty-meter circle, the half pass, the shoulder in, and the turn on the forehand are some of the movements that are combined together to make a certain test. The tests are arranged in a hierarchy of difficulty. The lower the level, the easier the test. First Level has much simpler movements than Second Level and so on, up to the higher levels. The lowest level is Training Level and one of the highest is Grand Prix, where a horse must perform pirouettes and trotting in place.

Salem learned fast, but I was even more impressed with how fast her owner was learning. At that point, I myself had almost given up showing my horse Shaman in favor of having Heidi ride him. The combination of Shaman and Heidi was so perfect that I had deferred to Heidi to ride him in shows. I had to admire Theodora's horsemanship as well as Salem's ability.

One day as Theodora and I happened to be washing our horses in crossties that were side by side, we started chatting.

"I have some friends back home who raise Morgan horses. I am sure you wouldn't know them since it is thousands of miles away in the state of Virginia," I said. "Their name is McGregor. I think he was even the President of the American Morgan Horse Association a couple of years back."

Theodora's face looked strange as she bent down to scrub Salem's left front hoof. "He's the one who made me lose my papers," she said under her breath.

I wasn't sure what she meant, but I could tell by her manner that the conversation was closed.

As time went by I was surprised by how remote Theodora always seemed. On her visits to the Ranch she seemed to avoid everyone except Heidi. She never wanted to chat the way most of the other owners did. I assumed she must be awfully busy. She would ride Salem and leave immediately afterwards.

A couple of months later after one of Shaman's lessons, Heidi brought up the subject of the horse show we were planning to enter that coming weekend.

"I hope you don't mind if Theodora and Salem go with us. She doesn't have a trailer, and it would be better to haul two horses than just one. It makes the load more even."

"Sure," I said. "The more the merrier."

In dressage shows the horses do not enter the ring together. Instead each horse is assigned a time to enter the arena alone to complete the required figures of the test. This is very similar to an Olympic gymnastics competition. The judge sits at a desk at the end of the arena and marks a test sheet with numbers from one to ten for each movement. She then calculates a total amount of points for the whole test. The horse with the highest total score wins the class for that level and gets the blue ribbon.

Shaman at First Level was at a different and higher level than Salem, who was just beginning Training Level. The two horses were not in competition with each other. There would be no hard feelings. On the contrary, both owners should be very supportive of each other.

Since it was only the second show Shaman had attended away from home, I was not surprised that this time he was nervous. He particularly did not like the dressage court that was covered and dark. It had huge mirrors on one side to allow the rider to evaluate his position.

Every time Shaman saw himself in the mirror, he shied. He was trying to avoid the strange horse that seemed to be coming at him from out of nowhere. Not surprisingly his scores were not good. He placed second in his tests instead of his usual first place.

On the other hand, Salem did very well. Because of her experience in shows over the last five years, she was cool as a cucumber. She and Theodora won both their tests.

I tried to ignore the fact that Theodora was an hour late arriving at the show. Because of this Heidi had been forced to occupy all her time with Salem. That had made Shaman jealous and may have contributed to his poorer performance. Like most Arabian horses, Shaman was very attached to anyone he considered as his own. He was jealous of any attention Heidi paid to another horse.

Theodora left in her own car after the show. I rode back to the Ranch with Heidi, pulling the trailer containing Salem and Shaman. I was tired from the long day of heat and dust. I asked Heidi in how many more shows was she planning to enter Shaman.

She replied that he needed six more successful tests from three different judges to qualify for the USDF (United States Dressage Federation) Horse of the Year award. She planned to enter him in the Arabian breed category. This meant that Shaman's scores on all his tests would be averaged and compared only to all other registered Arabian horses at his level. Heidi expected Shaman would do very well, since few Arabians are shown in this sport, which is dominated by the bigger warmbloods and Thoroughbreds. It would greatly limit the number of horses competing in each of his tests and give him a much better chance.

"Are you going to compete Salem in the tests for Morgan horses only?" I asked. "There should be even fewer Morgans than Arabians showing in this sport."

"No," Heidi replied. "When I approached Theodora about that, she told me something strange. Salem has been disqualified as a true Morgan by the American Morgan Association. I think it is just terrible."

"How in the world did that happen?" I asked.

"Well Theodora says that a friend that was showing her horse with her got jealous because Salem was always beating her. She questioned Salem's pedigree and said that she thought Salem was one quarter American Saddlebred."

This sort of thing has always been a problem in the world of expensive horse breeding. It was sometimes very hard to prove who the real father of a foal was. Since artificial insemination is widely used, it was especially easy to use the sperm from one stallion, and file registration papers claiming that another horse was the father. The solution to any doubts on the subject at the time was the same as to doubts of paternity in the human world—a blood test.

But at that time of Salem's mother's birth, blood testing was not required when registering a baby as a purebred member of a certain breed. There was no proof that Salem's mother was truly a purebred Morgan. So she could not compete in the show tests for Morgans only. She would have to go into the Open category, which would have many more competitors of all different breeds and it would be much harder for her to succeed.

Suddenly I remembered Theodora's words about Salem's lost papers.

Heidi continued. "The other woman claimed that one of Salem's grandfathers was a famous Saddlebred which is why Salem is so tall, fine-boned and showy for a Morgan. Theodora said that when she confronted Salem's breeder with the allegation and asked for a blood test on Salem's mother, the breeder answered that the mother was somewhere else temporarily. Can you imagine anyone letting it go at that? Why wouldn't anyone go find the mother and demand a blood test?"

"Maybe because Theodora was afraid the allegation was true," I proposed.

"Well, there was a board of inquiry called by the President of the American Morgan Association. They voted to disqualify Salem as a Morgan. It was terrible because a man had offered Theodora $70,000 for the horse and he removed his offer. Now she is hardly worth anything."

Now I understood what Theodora had said about my friend Mr. McGregor. He must have been head of the inquiry board that took away her papers.

"How sad that a little piece of paper can make so much difference," I said. "Any way you look at it, Salem is still a wonderful horse."

Salem and Shaman did not attend the next few shows together. Both Heidi and I were surprised and disappointed at Shaman's reaction and showing at the previous show. We had arrived at the show hours early to be in time for Salem's test. We agreed that his having to stand tied to the trailer for four hours waiting for his own test was too much to ask of a young horse just beginning his career. He had lost his edge by standing around too long. Also it was clear that he had just gotten mad at us about the whole thing.

We realized that Shaman required our complete attention in order to do his best. So if we wanted Shaman to win, we had to take him to the shows by himself. Luckily Theodora would be on vacation for a couple of months so there would be no conflict for Heidi about this.

Shaman's next show taught us something else. Again he did not do well and only took second place. That particular show was in an arena of a very different type from any in which Shaman had ever shown. It was a deserted place on the top of a very steep little mountain, far from the Ranch.

The dressage court was in a grove of redwoods and was outlined by a chain looped on short stakes instead of the usual thick white PVC pipe supported by white plastic buckets. Shaman could not keep his eyes off the chain. A horse as smart as he was saw it as something that was different and possibly dangerous if he tripped over it. Because of this his motions were jerky, instead of fluid as usual.

What was worse, at one point he actually shied badly and deviated from the course, something I hadn't seen him do since he had started his training a year ago. I was surprised that Heidi even stayed on him.

After the show as we were trailering the long drive home, Heidi and I came to a conclusion.

"I think I have made a mistake by skipping Training Level and starting to show Shaman at First Level. He has the ability to perform the First Level tests perfectly at home where he can concentrate on them. What he doesn't have is the experience going to the shows and being able to concentrate at that higher level," I admitted. "The fact is I think we are pushing him too hard."

"I agree," Heidi said. "From now on we should drop back and show him in Training Level."

The results were amazing. For the next few shows Shaman was back to his old invincible self. The only ribbons we brought back from shows were blue ones.

Then one day Heidi came to me and said, "I've got a problem. Theodora is back from vacation, and she has a bad case of shingles. She can't ride Salem in the show next weekend so she wants me to ride her myself. Also since both Shaman and Salem are entered in the same show, I will have to trailer them together. I hope you don't mind."

I did mind, but there was nothing I could do about it. "Shaman will just have to adjust," I said.

My husband John and I arrived at the Ranch at 5:00 AM the next Saturday morning in order to get Shaman ready for the hour trailer trip to the show in time for his ride at 8:00 AM. We unloaded our cooler from our car into the back of Heidi's truck. Our cooler was full of ice, iced tea, and the chicken salad sandwiches John had made.

It was chilly and I was wearing a jacket and riding gloves, which I knew I would remove by 10:00 AM as the temperature climbed. A typical show day started with temperatures in the low 50s and often ended in the high 90s.

Theodora lived near the show and would meet us there.

Heidi had already braided Salem's mane in the tight doubled-over braids required for a full mane. We were able to skip the braiding ordeal with Shaman because we had "roached" or cut his mane so short that it was only about an inch in length. He looked like one of the statues of ancient Greek horses. The protocol of dressage does not embrace romantic long manes flying in the breezes. As with everything else in the discipline, control is the rule.

As usual, Shaman was his easy charming self. He stepped up quickly into the two-horse trailer. He didn't even need to wear the heavy protective leg wraps necessary for most horses as he was always calm in the trailer and never seemed to hurt himself. I knew the reason why. He was always so busy concentrating on eating the hay in the small bin in the front under his nose that he didn't have time to get upset and thrash around. In fact, he loved to go into the trailer.

Salem was a different story. Both her legs and tail were wrapped securely as she tended to fret and rub them against the sides of the trailer. It took much persuasion and time to get her to go in beside Shaman, but finally we succeeded and we were off.

The trailer ride to that particular show was one of the most famous drives in the northern part of the state. It wound along two-lane country roads through the picturesque wine country. When we finally arrived, the view from the dressage court itself was a breathtaking one of hills covered with rows of grapes.

As I brushed and saddled Shaman, I realized something that had not occurred to me before. Heidi was riding Shaman and Salem one after the other in the same test at the same level. They were in direct competition with each other. One would win. One would lose.

Suddenly I was seized by a feeling that I hadn't felt since gym competitions in the sixth grade. I thought I couldn't stand it if Salem got a better score than Shaman. I was ashamed of myself, but I couldn't control it. This was a surprise as I considered myself a mature adult.

When we went to look at the arena, I said to John, "This dressage court has the worst footing I have ever seen. All the pebbles from the vineyards seem to be littered here."

"Yes, and Shaman's feet are so good he isn't wearing shoes. That could really be a problem." John replied.

"Oh Lord! I can't believe the perimeter is marked by a chain here. You know how that distracted him before."

Shaman was competing first. The rough footing was definitely a problem. As Heidi rode him around the warm-up arena, he seemed careful of his unshod feet and annoyed by the rocks. I was afraid the worst was about to happen.

My fears were confirmed when Heidi and Shaman entered the dressage arena for the first test. Shaman refused to go past the judges' stand at the end of court in his warm-up lap.

Then Heidi did something that showed why she was such a fabulous trainer. Instead of hitting Shaman with her whip and forcing him to go forward, she stopped and calmly leaning forward, asking the judge to let her ride the test out of competition. They would be graded, but the grade would not count. Halfway through the test, I saw Shaman relax, begin to concentrate and do well.

On the next test that followed and definitely counted, Shaman was spectacular. It was the best ride of his career so far. The crowd around me broke out into applause. I finally began to breathe again. Heidi dismounted, and we led Shaman back to the trailer to let him rest. We walked past Theodora heading toward the dressage court with Salem. Heidi handed Shaman's reins to me and got on Salem instead. She was ready for her turn on the other horse.

As I unsaddled Shaman, I could hear that, as usual, the crowd loved "La Belleza Negra." I couldn't bear to watch Salem's test, but I had no doubts that she had also done extremely well. She returned to join me and Shaman at the trailer after the test with an elated Theodora and Heidi.

My husband John and I had developed a pattern during the show season. Since he realized how nervous I was about the scores, he was always the one to go to the judges' stand to find out how we had done. I would wait to see him coming with the folded paper on which the test scores were written and hope to see his other hand holding a blue ribbon.

This time he seemed to take forever to return. At least twice the usual amount of time necessary for the judges to finish passed.

Finally I saw him coming. In his right hand he was holding two test papers, for both Shaman and Salem. In his left hand he had a blue ribbon and a red ribbon, for first and second place. There was a funny look on his face that caused my heart to stop. I was sure Salem had won the blue. I steeled myself to be generous and a good sport. After all, one of the basics of dressage was control.

"You'll never believe this, but it was a tie," John said, looking at both me and Theodora. Both Shaman and Salem got a score of 69.58 percent." He turned and handed the blue ribbon to me. The judge awarded the first prize to Shaman because he got a higher score of eight on his overall gaits. He won, but it was close."

"What's more," he said, "this is the high point for the whole show so far, so Shaman will probably get a multicolored ribbon and a prize for that."

Theodora turned slowly to me and said with a nice, controlled dressage smile, "Well, I think we can all agree that Heidi has done a fantastic job with these two horses."

"Yes," I agreed. "The trainer makes all the difference in the world. As far as I'm concerned, both of these horses won the high point in the show."

A few weeks later, Theodora moved Salem to another training barn that was thirty miles away. It was owned by a Western riding trainer.

I was sorry to see her go.

Salem may not have been a registered Morgan, but as far as I was concerned, she was still La Belleza Negra— the Black Beauty.

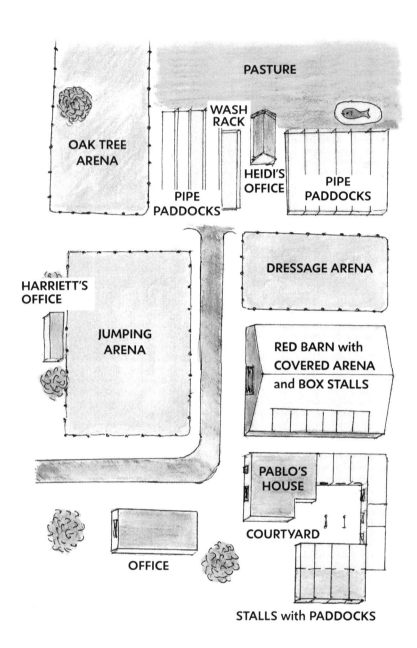

PASTURE

OAK TREE ARENA

WASH RACK

PIPE PADDOCKS

HEIDI'S OFFICE

PIPE PADDOCKS

HARRIETT'S OFFICE

JUMPING ARENA

DRESSAGE ARENA

RED BARN with COVERED ARENA and BOX STALLS

PABLO'S HOUSE

COURTYARD

OFFICE

STALLS with PADDOCKS

The Ranch

It was probably the very comfortable covered arena at the Ranch that had convinced me to choose this place over the many other local riding facilities. It comprised the major portion of the Red Barn. Its shelter allowed me to ride any time in spite of the weather. Its high-peaked roof kept out the rain in the winter and the hot sun in the summer. Its overhead lights even allowed riding during early morning hours or late into the evening. The rafters overhead had been the home of many pigeons until a pair of barn owls moved in. The Ranch's riders, no matter what type, loved to exercise their horses there.

Across from the Red Barn, the huge jumping arena was filled to the brim with strange obstacles of all sizes, descriptions and lengths. There were large boxes painted to look like brick walls or small picket fences with gay plastic flowers at the bottom. All were designed to challenge a horse's ability to clear them at speeds from a slow trot to a fast gallop.

Like many of the other older boarders, I considered myself too old and too wise to go tearing around over fences in the jumping arena. I preferred the more scientific, dignified, and possibly more demanding discipline of dressage. This is a safer form of horsemanship in which the horse executes certain difficult steps and gaits, controlled only by the rider's very slight movements. It is performed in a special dressage arena.

Every dressage arena has a low barrier marking its regulation-size court. Our dressage court was defined by a huge rectangle, twenty by sixty meters, of three-inch plastic pipe cut in ten-foot segments. These were supported about a foot above the ground by specially made gray plastic blocks with a grove in the top to hold the pipes loosely. If a horse kicked this boundary by mistake, no damage would be done to the court or the horse. A segment of pipe would pop out temporarily to be easily replaced after the ride. The level surface of the huge square was covered by inches of soft sand that the Ranch workers dragged smooth every morning by pulling a toothed harrow behind a tractor.

When not in one of the arenas, the horses at the Ranch resided in comfortable and clean accommodations. It was my job as Barn Manager to inspect these horse hotel rooms every morning when I arrived.

The Ranch had evolved over time. The three different types of equine accommodations: the box stalls, the pipe paddocks and the pasture had become subdivided by the three major categories of riders: dressage, hunter/jumper, and western. This was because the trainers of the very different styles each tended to want to keep all the horses in their care together for ease of handling and monitoring.

The hunter/jumper people training with Harriett occupied the Courtyard and the stalls in the Red Barn nearest her office. Most of the dressage horses were in the pipe paddocks at the top of the property close to

Heidi's office. The five or six horses in the pasture belonged to the few Western Riders at the Ranch.

The pasture was the cheapest accommodation on the Ranch. It was twenty-six acres of open space surrounded by a fence at the back of the property behind Heidi's Office. In the pasture there was a huge round communal water trough in which resided Columbus, the large red goldfish who had lived there for years. He had grown from only a couple of inches to almost a foot long. His job was to keep the algae under control, and he did it well.

Although they were in the Red Barn, the largest box stall accommodations were separated from the Covered Arena by a high wooden wall. This area was usually quite cool and comfortable. Most of the horses stood in their twelve-foot-square boxes with their heads hanging over the Dutch doors. The stalls had a six-inch deep layer of fresh cedar shavings from which the staff workers daily removed any manure or urine-soaked material and kept the floors very clean.

Additional box stalls were in a separate building. They were arranged with an open area in the middle like a medieval convent somewhere in the Mediterranean. Each of these stalls measured about ten feet square with a door in front. About half of these stalls had open windows covered by vertical iron bars in the back. This was called the Courtyard.

The most expensive accommodations were in a long exclusive row at the entrance to the Ranch. These were the box stalls, opening onto a twenty-foot long, open, private yard fenced in by four vertical iron pipes. In this best of both worlds, a horse could stay inside during the rain but stand in his yard paddock on nice days and enjoy the sun. The stalls were covered with bedding material. Some of the neater horses always walked out of their stalls onto the dirt of their private yards to relieve themselves.

Shaman lived in the mid-priced accommodations, the Pipe Paddocks. Each of these areas consisted of twelve side-by-side open stalls about ten by twenty feet composed of the same four vertical pipe fences. They were covered with corrugated iron sheets for protection from the rain. If the roofs had been removed, these open stalls would have resembled giant parallel playpens for horses.

I knew that my Shaman preferred his open pipe paddock to a small, enclosed box stall because he had spent his first three years of life in a pasture. Here he still had a sense of open space as well as the herd comfort of neighbors on each side that could be touched and smelled. He and his friend Denim often dozed with their heads together over the top of the bar separating them.

I sat on the porch of the trailer that was our office with my bird glasses focused on one of the apple trees in the guest area of the Ranch. A split rail fence enclosed this grassy area with its three plastic picnic tables with attached benches.

There was a large knothole about ten feet from the ground in one of them. Every few minutes or so a patch of bright blue appeared and flashed away from the trunk. A pair of bluebirds had appropriated this tree as a place for a nest. Several weeks earlier, I had noticed them bringing sticks and bits of hay, then disappearing inside the hole. Then for days I saw only occasionally the vivid male sitting on a branch nearby. I was afraid they were not going to stay.

But today the constant activity told me that the apparent disappearance of the female had been due to her sitting on the eggs. Now they were making regular trips with bugs and worms to feed their babies.

I compared each morning to my previous twenty-five years. Instead of putting on pantyhose and commuting to an office in the city to sit at a desk, I was working at an equestrian facility that boarded horses in a lovely rural valley. It was a wonderful change.

Mamma Kitty

Mama Kitty was one of the silent animal victims of divorce. She was brought to the Ranch when the owner, Janet, left her husband of twenty years and moved into an apartment that did not allow pets.

Although ranches may seem like cat heaven to many independent felines who grow fat on mice, sleep snugly on haystacks, and run merrily along the rails of the riding rings, Mama Kitty didn't fit in. She was a small British shorthair with delicate paws and striped fur of a color that could best be described as pale peach.

She was very shy, but if she liked you, she would sit quietly, tilting her round little face to follow your every move. In short, Mama Kitty was a house cat in every respect, completely unsuited to be a barn cat.

There were three barn cats at the Ranch, and they were all very different. Thin Smokey with short gray fur floated like a shadow in the expensive Courtyard area, where the horses lived in white wooden stalls around the central atrium reminiscent of a medieval convent in southern France.

Smokey, hardly more than a kitten herself, had appeared one day very pregnant and had immediately given birth. She was occasionally fed by the hunter-jumper people, whose Courtyard she kept free from mice.

Abner had been at the Ranch the longest, through two sets of owners to be exact. He was a large brown and black tabby. His massive head and shoulders had certainly discouraged attacks from skunks or other wild creatures that might visit the Ranch at night. His territory was the Pipe Paddocks on the hill where the more social and less pampered horses lived. As a whole he was the cat of the dressage faction since these stalls were closest to the dressage court and Heidi's office.

In spite of his rough looks, Abner was too picky to eat dry cat food and ate only the expensive cans given to him by the dressage riders. He resembled a Hanoverian or other warmblood horse with his bulk and slow controlled movements. There was no casual hacking around for Abner: he moved as though in a perpetual dressage test. He slept warm on a green blanket on top of the feed bins in the dressage tack room.

Casey—or "la gata negra"—as the men who were the principal help at the barn called her, claimed the Red Barn as her home. She was very fluffy and very fat, as the barn was a natural home for mice. She slept ten feet above the ground on the fortress of the oat hay pile, which protected her not only from the wild creatures, but from Abner who considered himself chief cat at the Ranch.

I had made it my own job to make sure that Casey got fed. She had stayed at the office with me when Janet had first brought her to the Ranch after she had been found at some of Janet's rental property. When I arrived at the barn every morning, Casey left her oat hay castle to come to greet me and ask politely for her breakfast.

Mama Kitty's first problem when she arrived at the

Ranch was that she was a house cat who had never seen a mouse, much less eaten one. The second was that there was no territory left for her to occupy. The three main areas of the Ranch were already taken. The Courtyard was Smokey's, the Red Barn was Casey's, and the dressage court and tack room belonged to Abner.

So Mama Kitty stayed around the office.

The office was a trailer of the type used on a construction site. As offices at horse barns go, it was very comfortable. Its walls were plastic pine paneling, and the chairs and rug were the brown and orange of cheap modern furniture. There were two large desks and a work area for the computer and printer along one wall. On the top of the bookcase was a digital clock radio whose large red numbers kept us punctual and which was usually playing hits of the 1960s.

The best part of the office was the large chart on the wall which depicted the layouts of all the stalls in the Courtyard, Red Barn and Pipe Paddocks, with a sticker for each horse showing its home. It was my job to update these stickers as horses arrived or left or were moved from stall to stall. The heavy winter rains would cause me to change it daily as certain stalls invariably flooded, and their tenants were moved temporarily to the closest dry spot.

The office even had an effective heater and air conditioner, which kept Janet, me and Mama Kitty quite comfortable.

Janet and I were glad to have Mama Kitty with us when we worked on the computer or did our business inside. She had nice manners and was good company. She became very fat from too much food and too little exercise as do many people who stay in offices for hours each day.

The problem came when the office began to smell very bad. I noticed the bad smell from the first time I walked into the office, but I was able to ignore it. Even the dirtiest equestrian with manure coated boots and a sweaty T-shirt would usually sniff the air as she walked in and with a scowl ask me how I could stand it in there.

It had been clear to me from the beginning that the bad smell was Winston. Winston was an ancient cocker spaniel of about the same peach color as Mama Kitty who had also been made semi-homeless by Janet's imminent divorce. In Winston's case, Janet had braved the apartment management by keeping Winston in the apartment at night. However, she was afraid to leave him alone there during the day as his control in matters relating to the toilet was beginning to weaken.

Consequently, Winston spent his days in the office with us.

Winston's eyes were clouded by cataracts. He was stone deaf and his behind was covered by a disgusting mass of warts. He was not a pretty sight, but worst of all, he smelled terrible. No amount of dog baths could erase his odor. To my mind, although I would certainly have chosen to share the office with Mama Kitty over Winston, I had to admire Janet's compassion for Winston's condition.

One day as Janet and I were working to update our files, the door to the office slammed open abruptly. In walked Howard, Janet's ex-husband and co-owner of the Ranch. His thin lips were compressed together in a hard line. He was not in a good mood.

"This place stinks!" he sniffed. "It can't be good for business for the office to smell so terrible. Janet, you ought to get that cat out of here."

I knew that Janet had a hard time asserting herself with Howard, so I gathered up my courage to reply. "I don't think it's Mama Kitty who smells bad, Howard. It's Winston. He's so old, and dogs always smell before cats do. Besides, it smelled bad in here before we started letting Mama Kitty spend the night."

He ignored my rational explanation. "Look," he snapped. "I have just spent half a day with the guy from the county health department with a complaint from one of the neighbors about the odor from the manure pile. There is no reason why we have to have a smelly cat box in the office as well."

So Mama Kitty was the unwitting victim of Winston's horrible smell. She was banished from the office at night, and she was now supposed to learn to be a barn cat.

Mama Kitty lasted about a week outdoors. At first she would be waiting for me outside the office each morning, but eventually she cowered under the office even during the day. Something had scared her badly.

Finally she disappeared altogether. I kept calling her and looking for her each morning, but she was nowhere to be seen. I accepted the fact that she had not been able to survive and that I would never see her again.

About two weeks later I was sitting at the desk helping a prospective boarder fill out a release agreement. I was shocked to see Mama Kitty walk into the office and go straight to her food bowl. I got up abruptly and hurried to open a can of her favorite cat food.

If it had not been for her pale peach fur, I would not have recognized her. She was terribly thin as if she had not eaten at all during the time she was gone. She gobbled the food I gave her in large gulps.

The worst of her condition was a hole in her left hip the size of a silver dollar. Its edges were blackened with necrotic tissue. I couldn't believe that Mama Kitty was alive, much less eating.

At the time Janet was away visiting her son in Los Angeles, but she had given me specific instructions that if anything happened to any of the animals, I should call the vet down the road. As soon as she finished eating, I grabbed Mama Kitty and got into my car with her in my arms.

When the vet's receptionist saw her, she immediately called him from the back of the hospital. Mama Kitty didn't fight as I held her on the examination table. As the vet touched her, she actually began to purr.

The vet shook his head with awe. "A person with a similar wound would probably be in shock. I looks like Mama Kitty has a large abscess from a puncture wound where she was bitten."

"She probably hid until she was able to open the abscess and allow it to drain," I postulated.

"I'll have to cut out a large portion of her skin to get rid of the dead tissue before I can sew it back together."

"Do you think she'll make it?" I faltered.

"Chances are good that she will recover, but . . ." Here he looked me straight in the eye, "it will be expensive."

"How much?"

"About $650."

Mama Kitty tilted her round little face up at me. "Go ahead," I said.

Two days later I went back to the vet's to pick her up. Mama Kitty was very unhappy as the vet brought her out to me in his waiting room. Around her neck was a large plastic cone. A row of about twenty stitches stretched across her naked left hip.

"This is to keep her from pulling the stitches out with her teeth." he explained.

Mama Kitty didn't like her Elizabethan collar one bit. She tried to scratch it off and jerked her head violently from side to side. When we put her down on the floor, she raced around and jumped crazily straight up in the air.

"I am afraid she will do more damage to herself with her collar than without it." I ventured.

When the vet removed the device, Mama Kitty immediately relaxed, turned and looked at her wound. She tried one stitch with her sharp little teeth, winced and gently licked her wound instead.

In spite of my fear of Janet's concern with money, I charged the exorbitant bill of $650 to the Ranch and took the invalid back home.

That was the end of Mama Kitty's apprenticeship as a barn cat. In order for her to recuperate, she of course had to be kept inside the office at night. But what should be done about Winston? Mama Kitty was in danger of reopening her incision by jumping up on the desk or computer to escape from him.

Since he was obviously disturbing the precious invalid, Winston was banished permanently during the day to the dog kennel next door to the vet's.

Not surprisingly, as soon as Winston was gone, the bad smell disappeared.

So Mama Kitty took on her new and most prestigious role as office cat.

Soon after Janet returned, Howard walked into the office. "Is that cat still here?" he asked.

"She is," Janet replied. "Any cat who cost $650 to repair is much too valuable to leave outside."

This time Howard was forced to listen to reason.

After that, Mama Kitty slept on top of the computer most of the time. She became very fat again. As she sat on the desk watching me talk on the phone, I noticed that the pale pink stripes on her left hip were crooked, like a seam in a piece of striped material cut apart and hastily stitched back together again.

I was glad she liked me enough to let me share her office.

Buster

I was shocked when I saw Bobbie Dayton for the first time. The tiny elderly lady who walked into the Ranch office did not match the strong vibrant voice on the phone that had reserved spaces for two horses.

In front of me stood a fragile little woman less than five feet tall with curly grey hair instead of the solid equestrian I had expected. She looked better suited to a bridge table than a horse ring. She seemed to be in her sixties or seventies, but I learned later that she was over eighty. A pair of grey riding pants hung loosely on her thin frame and were stuffed into black jumping boots that seemed much too large for her. By her side was a rather plump old man leaning heavily on a thick oak walking stick.

"I have the horses outside in the trailer," she said in a forceful voice. "This is Sam, my husband."

As we walked out of the office, I felt the unfamiliar feeling of towering over someone, since I am barely five foot two. She opened the back doors of the horse van to reveal one tall grey horse's behind and another short reddish chestnut one.

When she started to unload the grey horse, pandemonium broke loose. The huge horse came crashing out backwards. I couldn't believe this animal belonged to her. I had expected a calm old horse suitable for an old lady, but this horse acted more like a nervous two-year-old being led to the starting gate at the racetrack.

I was afraid that she would be jerked off the ground, but Bobbie held on to the lead rope firmly as she led the agitated creature into his paddock.

"He's a little high strung," she confided. "But I've always liked my jumpers that way."

Not knowing what to expect next, I walked back to the trailer to watch her unload the small chestnut horse. He backed out calmly and looked around. His big brown eye, his dished nose and small pointed ears told me that he was a purebred Arabian.

But his short stocky build told me clearly that he was a descendant of one of the old bloodlines before big-money breeders and the entertainment world had "improved" the breed with flashy temperaments and slender bodies.

"This is Buster," she explained. "He's my new horse. I decided to buy him after I was riding him on the trail recently. I leaned over too far to open a gate and fell off. He just stood there quietly looking at me. That's a good trail horse, I said to myself. Just what I need now that I am older."

Buster quietly followed Sam, who was lurching along on his cane, into his new paddock.

"You should see all of Bobbie's trophies," Sam said proudly." She used to be one of the most famous hunter-jumper riders in the area. She always competed at the big yearly show at the Horse Palace each fall. She could jump fences over six feet tall."

The next few weeks I watched from a distance as Bobbie and Sam settled into the life of the Ranch. I held my breath each time I saw them lead the grey Thoroughbred out to one of the turnouts. I feared he would knock down one or both of them with his nervous movements. Although this never happened, the horse's actions seemed to become more erratic with time instead of more calm, as would be expected.

The climax came when I received a call from Pablo, the stableman, in the middle of the night. The grey horse had fallen down on the ground in his paddock and was rolling. The vet had been called because of this unmistakable symptom of severe colic.

When I arrived at the office the next morning, Janet informed me that the horse had been put down. The body had already been removed. An autopsy revealed that a huge internal cancer was the cause of death.

Later that day I was surprised by Bobbie's sanguine attitude.

"I suspected something serious was wrong with him. He just got crazier and crazier. At least I have Buster left," she confided.

Now, for the first time, we at the Ranch got a chance to see Bobbie riding. First, she and Sam would take their time saddling Buster in his stall.

They did not use one of the crossties like most of the boarders at the Ranch. This meant that instead of being securely fastened by chains on either side of his halter as the saddle was placed on his back, Buster was standing freely during these preparations. Only the most confident rider with the most trustworthy horse would tack up a horse that was not tied in some way.

When the saddle and bridle were on, Sam would lead

Buster from the paddock. Then he would bring forward a garden chair of the aluminum frame and woven plastic strip variety that he would place at Buster's side. Bobbie would climb up on the wobbly chair and mount. I was more afraid the chair would tip over on the uneven ground than I was that Buster would move causing Bobbie to fall.

Neither happened. Buster would freeze and stand without moving a single muscle until Bobbie was safely in the saddle. Then Sam would remove the chair, and horse and rider would proceed slowly down the path past the paddocks to one of the riding arenas.

I began to realize that all of my fears that Bobbie would get hurt were groundless. She was a wonderful rider, sitting securely in the saddle with almost no visible movement, no bouncing, no jiggling legs.

Perhaps this was because after the first few days she and Buster almost never trotted. A trot is the gait with a two-beat footfall that bounces the rider the most. Instead Bobbie taught the little red horse to go directly from the walk to a canter, the smooth motion that resembles sitting in a rather fast rocking chair. Since a horse normally increases its speed by going from the walk to the trot before reaching the canter, this took a lot of patience on Bobbie's part and much cooperation from Buster.

Bobbie and Sam were also very sensible about the weather. They only appeared at the Ranch in the evenings after the hot summer sun had set and the air had cooled. This was possible because of the tall stadium-type lights around the jumping arena. If I was working late in the office, I could see Bobbie riding as late as 9:00 PM. I wondered how she had such stamina.

"Now I have seen everything," intoned Heidi, shaking her head as I entered her office.

"What?" I asked expecting to hear of some crazy bareback stunt from one of our younger riders.

"Bobbie has taught him to pee in a bucket!" she laughed.

"Sam?" I replied, shocked.

"No, of course not," she answered, "Buster."

"That's impossible."

"Well, she has. She says it keeps from having to replace the wood savings on the floor of the stall so often and saves her money."

I would not have believed it had I not seen it for myself the very next day. Immediately after riding and removing his saddle, Bobbie put Buster back in his paddock. The tiny lady placed a large bucket under the horse who immediately urinated and filled it to the brim. She then carefully emptied the contents on the ground far from the stall and the other horses.

Bobbie's concern with stall cleanliness pleased me very much because Shaman's paddock was next to Buster's. They got along well except for one incident.

Pablo, the head stable hand, came to me complaining, "La Viejita is leaving open the paddock of the little red horse." La Viejita, or the little old lady, was the nickname that all the workers had attached to Bobbie.

"I'll talk to her," I promised, although I doubted that anyone as careful around horses would be so lax. I actually suspected that Sam, whose memory was not the greatest, was responsible.

When I arrived at Buster's stall, I found Bobbie and Sam working diligently to install an extremely complicated new lock on the paddock door.

"Absolutely horse-proof!" grinned Sam.

"You mean Buster has been opening his own lock and letting himself out?"

"No, he can't reach it, but Shaman can. I finally caught your little varmint playing with it with his mouth until he got it open. Since he can't get to his own lock I guess he figured he might as well do a favor for Buster," Bobbie interposed.

From the way she spoke, I could tell that Bobbie highly approved of Shaman's intelligence. I didn't doubt her conclusion. I remembered how Shaman's mother had required a total of five locks of different types in different places to prevent her opening the gate of her pasture.

Once again I was impressed with Bobbie's savvy about horses. This impression did not change for the next three years.

Sometimes Sam came to the Ranch alone to take care of Buster. He would give the paddock an extra cleaning even though the Ranch cleaned each stall daily. Sometimes he would putter around with a hammer, fixing anything that might be loose and therefore dangerous.

One day, I saw Sam, alone, leading Buster out to one of the turnouts. This was a large fenced-in exercise area designed to give a horse more room to move around than its stall. I had to take a second look. It was hard to tell who was leading whom.

Sam used his cane with the curved handle linked through Buster's halter to support himself. He leaned heavily on the free end of the cane holding it perpendicular to the ground. Then they proceeded at a snail's pace along the path to the turnout. With almost every step, Buster would stop and wait for Sam to shuffle forward. The little horse was clearly holding the old man up.

One day I realized that I hadn't seen Bobbie or Sam for several days. I decided to ask around the Ranch to see if anyone knew what was up. Perhaps one of the people who came to the Ranch mostly only in the evenings, when Bobbie and Sam were usually there, would be able to tell me something.

As I returned to the Ranch after my supper that night, I was surprised to see Ralph, the owner of a huge black Hanoverian named Victor, leading Buster to one of the turnouts.

"Didn't you know?" he was surprised. "Bobbie had a heart attack last week."

"Who is taking care of Buster?" I asked.

"We all are," he answered. "Jane, Jason's owner, turns him out in the mornings, and I turn him out again at night. He is fine, but I think he misses Bobbie."

This arrangement continued for a couple of months. Every morning and most evenings as I drove past the Ranch, I could see Buster standing quietly by himself in the turnout closest to the road.

Then one night when I was staying late in the office to get out the monthly billing, I looked out of the window to see Bobbie and Sam walking toward Buster's paddock.

Bobbie seemed to have shrunk to an even smaller size if possible. I watched as they saddled Buster as usual. Then instead of bringing out the lawn chair they had used as a mounting block, I saw Ralph and his pretty wife lift Bobbie up into the saddle as Buster stood patiently.

The tiny lady seemed almost about to fall off, but she regained her balance, picked up the reins and headed down the path toward the jumping arena. I ran to hold the gate to the arena open for them, but Bobbie just smiled and rode by me. She turned instead toward the path leading around the barn.

I think we'll just ride around the place a little today," said Bobbie with a grin. "We're a little out of shape."

Some people think horses are dumb animals. Real horse lovers know differently. I know that I saw a look of quiet concern and worry in Buster's big eye as he picked his way carefully around the barn.

I knew that Bobbie would be safe as long as she was on his back.

Foster

DOGS MUST BE KEPT ON A LEASH AT ALL TIMES

This was one of the strictest rules on the Ranch. Not only did good horse sense dictate this leash law, the Ranch's insurance policy required it.

There was a very good reason for this restriction. A horse is instinctively an animal of prey. When threatened by a possible predator, it can react by moving very quickly. This can result in a serious fall for an unprepared or unskilled rider. It can also mean a crushed foot for anyone standing in between the startled horse and its desired escape route. Although most horses are not really afraid of individual dogs, they often cannot control their reflex impulse to run when surprised by any dog running up fast from behind.

The exception to the leash law was that our insurance allowed for one dog. This canine was designated as the resident Ranch Dog. When I first came to the Ranch, the honor of Ranch Dog was enjoyed by Winston, the owner's ancient, smelly, blond Cocker Spaniel.

As Winston was entirely blind from cataracts and crippled with arthritis, the only danger he posed to any rider was if he happened to stumble under a horse because he couldn't see it. Since Winston almost never left the office, this was not very likely.

When Winston finally died, Janet did not replace him. This meant that the Ranch was without an official dog for a year or so. During that time in accordance with the rules, all of the horse owners continued to keep their own dogs carefully leashed and tied to a tree or fence while riding.

Soon after Heidi got married, she and her new husband adopted a puppy as a substitute for the real baby they planned to have in a year or two. The puppy they chose was an Australian Shepherd. He was unusual in his color. He was not the standard black and tan or grey brindle, but instead was tan with white markings like the old respected Scottish collie of the Lassie variety. This non-regulation color and the fact that the iris of one of his eyes was half blue and half yellow had made the price of the dog very much agreeable to the young couple. They named him Foster after the Australian lager, in honor of his heritage.

From the minute she first got him, Heidi refused to leave Foster alone at home. The round, fluffy, honey-colored puppy followed close behind her as she went around her business at the Ranch. At first the horses in her care were very careful not to step on the poky little ball of fur. As Foster matured into a strong young dog, they seemed immune to his cavorting around.

Every morning Foster would celebrate the day by running up and down the Ranch as fast as he could. He would settle down after an hour or so and lie along the low white plastic rail in the arena, watching as Heidi rode one of her charges. None of the horses gave him a second glance as they worked, even though he lay only inches from where their hooves passed. When Heidi went to get another horse from its stall, Foster would race ahead of her at top speed.

Even the Ranch cats seemed to accept the fact that Foster was harmless, though at first he would steal the cat food left in the bowls on the front porch of the office. Eventually Heidi taught him to leave the cats and their food alone. Mama Kitty would give him a disapproving glare as he raced up to her porch and froze within inches of her nose to watch her eat. After a few minutes, Foster would race back to Heidi's side without being called.

I had mixed feelings about Foster. On the one hand, as manager of the Ranch, I felt obliged to enforce the rules and tell Heidi that in order to prevent an accident, Foster should be on a leash. On the other hand, I could see that all of the horses seemed to be used to him and that Heidi was supervising his antics closely. I really didn't think that Foster presented a problem to anyone. I decided to ignore the problem until Janet or Howard brought it up.

The main reason I could never bring myself to talk to Heidi about Foster was that every time I would be about to complain about him, he would do something so funny that it would diffuse my righteousness.

Foster was a little thief at heart. He could not resist picking up anything that he fancied and trotting off with it.

"Where is my sponge?" asked one of the ladies over her shoulder as she bent down to search through her portable plastic tack carrier in the crossties by her big gray horse. "I need to wipe off the sweat on his forehead under where his bridle was."

"Guess who?" I said, as we both turned to see Foster lying under a tree nearby, chewing on the missing sponge.

"Foster, give that back," commanded Heidi as she walked over to take the sponge from the dog and hand it back to its owner.

We all three laughed as Foster looked up as if devastated by the loss of his new toy. From then on sponges seemed to disappear constantly at the Ranch.

One of my major responsibilities at the Ranch was to clean the indoor bathroom that was next to the entrance to the Courtyard stalls. Most of the boarders or students going to get their horses would give me their condolences as they passed. Maid work wasn't their idea of a good time.

Surprisingly, I actually looked forward to this cleaning job. The windowless, concrete-floored restroom was the coolest spot on the Ranch. It got very little serious use. Also it was very rewarding to see the white porcelain fixtures shining up at me after I removed the thick coating of dust that is part of any riding establishment.

I always started my routine by donning my plastic gloves. Then I removed the plastic toilet brush from behind the bowl and placed it outside the door in the Courtyard until I was ready for it. I continued sweeping and polishing and finally reached out from the door for my implement.

It was gone. I looked all around but couldn't find it.

"Am I getting senile and forgetting where I put things? Who would have taken the toilet brush?" I asked Heidi as she led Bravo, one of her big dressage horses, past the restroom for his daily workout.

Slowly I remembered that wherever Heidi was, Foster

was not far away. I turned a half circle to the left. There, thirty feet away, in front of Bravo's stall, was my toilet brush. Foster had deserted it in his rush to escort Heidi out to the arena. I should have known.

For my own part, Foster cost me a riding crop about once a month. I always carried a crop. I never used it on my darling Shaman, but I had gotten in the habit of having one in my hand during the fifteen years I had spent previously as a trail rider.

It had all started when a serial killer terrorized the trails of our peaceful county. He killed at least four hikers before being caught. My riding companion and I were afraid that our horses were so friendly that they would not run from any threatening individual, so we started carrying whips. We hoped this would make them move away quickly if necessary. At worst we could beat the killer over the head if he attacked us. I also think that the crop made me feel more secure with something in my hand besides the reins. Being on top of a fast moving horse can be a very unstable experience, especially as one grows older.

Each time I tacked up and led Shaman out to our lesson with Heidi, Foster would follow me, jumping up, trying to grab my crop. If he succeeded, he would run off shaking it as if to kill it. By the time someone retrieved the whip, it was often broken with both ends drooping at a ninety degree angle.

At other times if I laid my crop down to tighten the girth before mounting, Foster would have time to disappear with it before Heidi could catch him. Then I would probably never see that particular crop again. Luckily, crops are not too expensive. Foster enjoyed the game so much that it was impossible to get mad at him. I also suspected that Shaman was quietly cheering him on.

Not that I was always so tolerant of Foster. Once when Heidi and I were taking Shaman to a show, I rebelled against Foster coming along. When we were ready to leave, I opened the driver's side door to my ancient Ford truck. In hopped Foster.

He carefully squeezed under the legs of Heidi and my husband John, the two passengers already in the single seat. I would have been the fourth occupant. A wiggly, not too clean-smelling dog was too much to add to the already crowded group. And this show was at least a three hours drive away from the Ranch.

I was already in a nervous state. This was before we cut Shaman's mane short. As usual, Shaman had not been cooperative about having his mane braided. He had resisted my efforts as much as I had always fought against having my own pigtails plaited when I was a little girl.

The situation was made worse because I had declined Heidi's advice to "pull" Shaman's mane so that it would only be about four inches long. Instead its current length was almost twenty inches. I felt that he was entitled to the long beautiful thick black mane that was his heritage as a purebred Arabian horse. The problem was that the long hair became almost impossible to braid neatly and loop into the disciplined coif required for a show.

Hanging onto the mane of a stamping, impatient horse while balancing on a chair for an hour at 5:30 AM is not the way to acquire a good disposition. This is especially true if you know that you have to hit the road by 6:00 AM.

"We are not going to take HIM!" I barked to Heidi as

I scowled at Foster.

"He wants to go," she said.

"There's not enough room for all of us," I countered.

"You and John could take your car and I could drive the rig," she argued.

"Are you kidding? Take an extra car just so a dog can come along? Besides, he can't run loose at the show and we don't need anything else to keep up with." I was nearly hysterical.

"Okay, I'll have to take him home. He can't stay here without me all day."

"We'll be late," I wailed.

"I'll hurry," she said, her eyes wide as my usually calm nature exploded.

In spite of it all, we did make the show on time, and without Foster. Shaman won his usual blue ribbons. The day also resulted in one of my favorite photos of me with Shaman looking very neat and tidy as though he always wore braids on Saturday.

But I couldn't stay mad at Foster for long. The next morning I led Shaman into the arena at the Ranch for a lesson. I noticed that someone had attached one of those silver-colored helium filled balloons with a smiley face to the door of Heidi's office. It was attached to a short stick that was stuck through the office door handle.

Needless to say Foster couldn't resist trying to steal the balloon. From my viewpoint on Shaman's back I could see him finally pull it loose. He came trotting toward Heidi who was sitting in a white plastic chair beside the arena. The balloon floated along bouncing in the air behind the perky yellow dog.

As Foster stopped to rest, it bobbed down and bumped

him on the behind. A frightened Foster took off still holding the balloon. It appeared to him to be chasing him down the road to the barn. Luckily, Shaman did not spook at this strange apparition running in front of him. It was a good thing, because both Heidi and I were laughing helplessly.

In spite of his pestering, or maybe even because of it, I always felt that Foster really had a special fondness for me. He often gave a single gruff bark at anyone approaching him and Heidi. Yet whenever he saw me coming, his ears would perk up. Then he would freeze until I acknowledged his presence by calling his name or stooping down to meet him. Finally, he would come charging to greet me with his tongue hanging out and his short tail wagging his whole body.

Even I had to agree. Foster had become the official Ranch Dog.

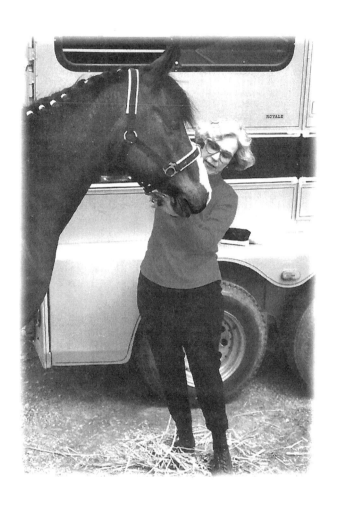

Lipizzaner Ladies

The truck with the horse trailer attached was parked in the Ranch driveway in front of the Courtyard stalls. It was ready to take four ladies to a fancy resort and horse facility on the coast, about one hundred miles south of the Ranch.

Heidi and I leaned back in the cab of the truck trying not to laugh. In front of us stood one of the funniest sights we had ever seen. The horse looked like she was about to attend a Halloween party dressed as an ice hockey player. Her ears stuck out from a bulky leather helmet. The bottom half of each of her legs was wrapped in thick padding. It was almost impossible to tell that underneath all the protection was a beautiful white mare.

It was Nita, a Lipizzaner, a member of the breed made famous by the performing horses of Vienna. For most people, the sight on television of these gorgeous creatures with their uniformed riders is the first introduction to the art of dressage.

Nita's owner, Jennifer, opened the truck door. In her designer jeans and bright geometric print blouse, she looked the part of the oil and watercolor artist she was. I had met her once before, but knew her only as one of the

Lipizzaner owners at the Ranch. There were only two of them. I knew the other, Laura, well. She and her husband often accompanied me and my husband to plays in the city.

Jennifer explained to Heidi and me, "Maybe I overdid the padding, but I don't want her to hurt herself in the trailer. She is much too valuable."

Instead of her usual tight riding pants, Heidi was wearing a pair of faded jeans. She nodded in agreement, "Especially if she gets approval to become a brood mare."

"Explain it to me again. Exactly what is this trip all about?" I squirmed. My own jeans felt a little snug because I was crammed into the small back seat.

"The head veterinarian of the Spanish Riding School in Vienna, which is the home of the breed, is in the U.S. deciding if a horse bred in this country stacks up as a true Lipizzaner," Heidi answered. "They have to be physically judged to see if they make the grade and look like the ones in Vienna."

Jennifer responded, "If Nita gets a good report, that makes her a much more valuable horse for me. If she passes the test, I will be able to sell her babies for thousands more."

"What kind of test is it?" I asked.

"Usually for a test they ask the owner or a trainer to hold the horse in front of the judge. Then they walk and trot the horse in the pattern of a triangle so the person judging can see it from all angles. That is the test for conformation, a horse's body shape."

"So that is the reason we are taking these horses to a fancy riding establishment near the coast," I concluded. "We are going to meet this guy from Vienna and get his approval."

"We and about thirty other Lipizzaner owners. All of them have babies born in this country and want to get official approval. I really appreciate you ladies helping me do this," Jennifer shook her head and smiled. "Come on. Let's load her up."

Heidi answered, "We have to wait until Laura loads her gelding, Bogart, first. She is taking him too, and I am going to ride him. He is older, and I have been showing him. Several other horses will be ridden as a sort of exhibition show for the crowd."

"It was great that Laura agreed to take her rig," she continued. " My truck and trailer are too old to make the trip. And her new one has a back seat so that all four of us can go."

As our trainer, Heidi was unofficially in charge. Even though she was much younger than Jennifer, Laura and I, she had the last say.

So after Laura and Jennifer had loaded their horses, we four horse ladies settled in. We shut the doors of the shiny red truck, and the heavily loaded horse trailer rolled out of the Ranch.

For a couple of hours we drove along the freeway. In spite of a load of a few tons of horse, the big trailer hummed along. Laura was driving her new twin cab pickup. Heidi rode shotgun. Jennifer and I, who were the smallest with the shortest legs, occupied the narrow back seat. Our close proximity was conducive to lots of chatting and laughing. Horse stories and close calls about riding dominated the conversation.

This is really fun, I thought.

After another hour, we realized that we should be heading over toward the ocean. The freeway would only take us down the middle of the state, but the location of the meeting was on the coast. I was holding the map.

"It looks like we could reach our goal quicker if we took this road here," I said, pointing to a thin line at a right angle to the freeway. "This road would take us to the coast and come out just above Stone Tree. Isn't that the place?"

"Sounds good to me," replied Laura, grasping the steering wheel firmly in her hands.

So we made a right turn at the next exit and headed west. The chatting and laughing continued for a few miles on the narrow two-lane road. Then I felt myself being pushed back into the seat as the trailer began to climb.

The hill we were on became steeper. We began to talk less as our pace became slower and slower. The truck was having a hard time pulling the weight of the trailer with its two horses up the grade. There was no place to turn around on the narrow road, as there was a drop-off on one side and a sharp rise on the other.

Finally there was complete silence. We looked at each other with fear as we all simultaneously imagined what might happen. What if we stopped climbing upward altogether? What if the whole rig started rolling backwards? The thought of what would happen to us and the horses was horrible. Laura gripped the steering wheel and kept going. I saw Heidi in the shotgun seat rigidly watching the road ahead.

Soon the truck was hardly moving at all. I felt a panicky tightness in my chest.

Then through the windshield between Laura and Heidi, I saw that we were almost to the top. When we cleared the ridge, the truck and trailer began to roll more freely again. Suddenly we all looked at each other and laughed.

"I was afraid we weren't going to make it," I said. "I have never prayed so hard in my life."

Next to me Jennifer was almost crying, "My poor horse, all that padding wouldn't have been enough. . . ."

Before she finished, we realized we had another, even bigger problem. As we descended the other side of the steep hill, the rig began to pick up speed. The weight that had been such a drag going uphill began to cause the opposite reaction going downhill.

We rolled faster and faster. I began to smell an odor like burning toast that I realized was the brakes. Laura's body was stiff as she gripped the steering wheel with one hand and strained to keep her left foot on the brakes. Now I had an awful picture of the rig jackknifing and hurling us to the bottom of the ridge.

"Hold on, Laura," Heidi said as calmly as when she was giving a beginner a riding lesson on a strange new horse. "You can do it."

For once in my life, I said nothing. I just braced against the back of the driver's seat and tried to breathe. The burning smell of the brakes was almost overpowering in the back seat.

It seemed like hours instead of the few minutes that actually elapsed until we reached the bottom of the grade. The rig began to slow down. At last we resumed our normal speed on flat ground.

Laura was able to pull her foot off the brake slowly and relax. The rest of us slumped back in our seats. Still nobody said anything.

"Next time I'll be the navigator," Heidi said. She turned around to look at me.

We all broke into hysterical laughter.

We were exhausted when we pulled into the grounds of Stone Tree. The rig rattled through an elaborate gate flanked by a life-size sculpture of a horse. At the end of a long private road, we arrived in front of a large, Spanish-style villa. Its pale stucco facade was surrounded by well-manicured plants and trees.

We walked through the arched, tiled entrance into a sumptuous reception area with floor to ceiling windows on three sides. Beautiful blue and gold tiles covered the bottom half of each wall. Shiny dark wood covered the floor and comprised the beams in the ceiling. In our jeans and heavy horse-proof shoes, we seemed ridiculously out of place.

"Are you sure this is the right place?" I whispered to Jennifer. She raised her eyebrows and shrugged in uncertainty.

Heidi went up to the desk. "We are with the Lipizzaner Association."

The clerk, in his expensive European-cut gray suit, searched through his book with his manicured fingers. "Ah, yes," he said. "You are in the Ranch House in the Seattle Slew room. It's down the drive to the right. You can't miss it."

As we walked back out to the rig, I tried not to step on the lovely blue Chinese rug with my dusty barn shoes.

We got back in the truck and continued along the private road. Soon we began to follow the type of wooden fencing that often surrounds horse property. Eventually we came to a large, gray, one-story building that resembled a farmhouse in Kentucky horse country. On its left was a huge barn with a row of twelve white horses staring at us over Dutch doors.

"This must be the place," Heidi said. "It looks like other Lipizzaner owners are already here."

We walked up the steps, crossed the big front porch, and went in. On each side of the entrance hall were doors marked with fancy lettered plaques, each with the name of a famous racehorse.

We found the door marked "Seattle Slew" and stepped into a comfortable suite. The living room was decorated in a cozy Western Ranch style with two big comfortable sofas. We walked past a small, well-stocked kitchen into a large bedroom with cheerful calico curtains over three large windows. Between two of them was a bed with a matching print bedspread.

"Isn't this great?" I asked as I fell into a big comfortable chair.

"Yes, but . . ." Laura said, looking at the bed. Then her shoulders drooped.

"But what?" Heidi asked.

"There is just one bed and there are four of us," she replied.

"Uh oh," we all answered in chorus.

"Don't worry about it," Heidi shrugged, "Who is going to have time to sleep? We can't leave those horses alone for long in a strange barn. In thirty minutes we have to be at the dinner barbeque. Afterward there will be a talk by the guy from Vienna in the bar over the barn, which will probably last until midnight. Then I have to be up at 5:00 AM to get the horses ready to be in the judging."

"You're right," said Jennifer, walking toward the door, "Let's go over to the barn and find someone to tell us which stalls are reserved for our horses. We should get them out of the trailer as soon as we can. I think I'll stay over there with Nita until time for the barbeque."

We did have time to change from our dirty jeans into clean clothes for dinner. Jennifer, the painter and clothes designer, put on one of her own creations, a stunning grey leather jacket with a portrait of Nita on the back. The flowing white mane stood out on the slate gray leather. The rest of us had on our best fitting pants and shiniest paddock boots.

When we left the house at dusk, we saw a crowd standing around a big barbeque pit in the stable yard. I recognized many familiar faces as they chatted over glasses of wine. There were several ladies I had seen competing against Shaman in shows and even a few show judges. Many held plates of beef and beans. Everyone was having a good time. Competition was forgotten. Over the background of country music, common interests and tales about horses were being traded.

After the hearty, fattening dinner, we all trouped up to the large room above the barn. On one wall was a long bar, like one you might find in a Western movie. A pool table and several poker tables were scattered around the room. Some people found seats, but most of us stood against the windows at the back.

A very attractive thin man with very blond hair in expensive, Eastern-style riding clothes and extremely high, black dressage boots began to speak with a heavy Austrian accent. He talked mostly about the Lipizzaner breed.

I already knew that only the stallions were trained to show. I found out that they are not even bred until they have reached one of the highest levels to insure that the offspring will possess the same capabilities. He said that the biggest current problem is one of inbreeding because the population is so small. I had guessed that was a problem because they were so exclusive.

During the question and answer period at the end of his talk, a woman with stylishly short hair stood up. I recognized her as a judge from one of Shaman's shows. Her slim figure testified to lots of early mornings and long days at dressage courts. She asked, "What is the worst mistake we make in the US in training our horses?"

"That's easy," he said. "In the US you start training them too early. You begin training horses at two or three years of age. In Vienna we would never do that. We wait until they are five or six so their bones are more mature."

The room fell silent. I imagined that we all felt a little guilty.

After all the wine and barbeque and inside information, we stumbled back to our suite. We were beat. I remember Heidi setting her alarm clock for 5:00 AM, only a few hours away.

The next thing I knew it was daylight. On the other side of the bed with me was Laura who was snoring slightly. Jennifer and Heidi were already gone. A pillow and blanket on one of the sofas in the living room showed someone had slept there. I didn't know who. I suspected that Jennifer had slept somewhere in the stable with Nita.

I was in the kitchen when Heidi walked in.

"I've got to get some more coffee before I die," she said.

"I'll make some breakfast," I offered.

"No need, they had coffee and sweet rolls at the barn," she said. "Most of the horse owners are already over there. Laura took the first shift watching the horses after the lecture, then Jennifer took over."

I began to feel a little guilty about my four hours of sleep. "If Shaman had been here, I would have been over there too," I offered.

"Don't worry about it, you'll get your turn later," she countered. "I've got to get my riding clothes on. The judging starts in a couple of hours and I want to warm up Bogart.

After we both had dressed, we went out to the barn. The morning air was cool and still. I was glad I had brought my warm barn jacket. Heidi's rather long formal black dressage riding coat must have felt good now, but by noon on a hot day it could be torture. Her high black boots made a formidable sound as we strolled down the front steps of the Ranch House.

Jennifer was waiting for us with Nita already cleaned up. Instead of a ridiculous ice hockey player, she looked like an advertisement for a Lipizzaner commercial on TV. The horse looked fresh and ready to go. Her white hair was spotless. On the other hand, Jennifer looked beat. The jacket and pants that were neat for last night's dinner were dirty and rumpled now.

"I never got to sleep at all," she complained, "But Nita is fine and that's all that counts. She really loved the horse in the stall next to her."

Laura arrived next, yawning. "I almost didn't wake up. But Bogart's ride time is not until eleven o'clock, so there was no hurry. I had better go and get him ready."

By eight o'clock, the area in front of the barn was crowded with people holding the reins of white horses. There were mostly ladies, but a few men were scattered here and there. I assumed they were probably husbands, as most amateur dressage riders are female. It was a beautiful sight with all the long manes and tails. It reminded me of pictures in a book of fairy stories.

In the middle of the crowd was a large empty space. The veterinarian from Vienna stood there holding a clipboard in one hand and a pen in the other. One at a time a horse was led in front of him. He stepped forward, then walked around and looked at it from all angles, making notes as he went. When he finished making his notes, the person leading the horse took the halter and asked the horse to walk and then trot in a large triangle.

This scene continued for three hours as horses were led out one by one to be evaluated. Luckily the Viennese vet liked Nita's looks and gave her high marks. Jennifer was ecstatic.

After the last horse had been led away, one of the ladies stepped forward and announced," We will now present a riding exhibition by one of our most successful horses and his trainer. Here is Bogart ridden by his trainer, Heidi."

Even in the absence of a dressage arena or music, Heidi put Bogart through his paces. They demonstrated half passes, in which the horse seems to move sideways instead of forward, and lead changes, in which the horse seems to be skipping. There was enthusiastic applause from all the onlookers. The man from Vienna smiled broadly through the whole performance. He obviously approved.

When Heidi finished, she rode Bogart back to where Laura, Jennifer and I were standing. With the reins in one hand, she leaned down and whispered, "Let's get out of here as fast as we can. There will be a line of trailers from here all the way to the highway."

We nodded in agreement.

"I'll go get our gear out of the room," I offered.

"Just one more thing," Heidi said looking down at me with a frown.

"What?" I asked.

"No short cuts this time, please," she grinned.

Scout

Scout arrived at the Ranch on a very cold day in late October. The wind blew leaves across our path as we led him down the row of pipe paddocks. Although it was the kind of a day that makes most horses skittish, he looked around very calmly and went without hesitation into the enclosure that was to be his new home.

I could see immediately that he was an old campaigner. His dull seal brown coat, rather plain head and lanky body identified him to me as one of those old Thoroughbreds who had survived not because of flashy looks, but because he was good to ride.

"What do you plan to do with him?" I asked. His owner, Susan, was a bleached blond whose actions and looks caused the word "bimbo" to pass through my mind.

"Oh, I don't know," she said, as she beamed at the handsome man with her who was closing the paddock door. "I have always wanted to own an ex-race horse ever since I was a little girl. I guess Henry and I will just take turns riding him."

"But do you jump, or are you into dressage, or maybe you'll just do some work on the flat?" I was beginning to have definite misgivings.

"Oh no," she replied, "maybe I'll take him out on the trail. I really haven't ridden much since I was a child. I saw Scout for sale when I was up in Reno and just couldn't resist buying him. He was so cheap."

"Has he ever been out on trails?" I asked. "Thoroughbreds aren't usually used as trail horses. Mostly on the trails around here you see Arabians, Morgans or Quarter Horses."

"Oh he'll learn," she said, breezily.

The feeling in the pit of my stomach grew heavier. As I looked at her long red sculptured fingernails, it was clear to me that she was definitely not a horsewoman. You don't have to be plain or unattractive to work with horses. I have seen attractive ladies set out on fifty-mile endurance rides down a mountain with perfectly applied makeup, even tons of mascara. For that matter one of the temptations of dressage is the stylish and impeccable outfit worn and the classiness of many of the lady riders.

But there is one dead giveaway that you work with horses. That is the condition of your fingernails. It is very difficult to keep long manicured fingernails while spending hours a week cleaning hooves, brushing a horse and especially buckling bridles and tightening girths. Most ladies who care for their horses eventually wind up with short fingernails. Since a new manicure may only last until the next ride, most horsewomen avoid them.

I left Scout's new home with a premonition of a coming disaster.

I heard about Susan's first and last ride on Scout about a week later when I was saddling up Shaman for a weekly lesson.

Heidi shook her head as she told me the details. "She hadn't been on him for two minutes in the ring before she tried to get him to canter. She started to bounce and lost her stirrup during the transition from the trot. The next thing I could see was her sitting on the ground. Of course Scout went running across the ring glad to be free."

I agreed. "Any experienced rider would have taken it slowly for the first time up with a new horse and only walked a while before trying anything faster. Who knows how long it has been since he was last ridden?"

Needless to say we didn't see much of Susan at the Ranch after that incident. Her enthusiasm for riding had disappeared completely, and Scout stayed in his paddock neglected. I would see him standing listlessly for days on end. The only contact he had with anyone was when the men brought his food twice a day. About two months after his arrival, we received word in the office that Susan wanted to move him to the much less expensive pasture.

About the same time that Scout was moved to the pasture, forgotten by his owner, Heidi acquired a new helper.

Most of the trainers had young girls working for them doing the necessary routine maintenance work for which the trainer was responsible. This included grooming the horse, such as brushing or washing it, and tacking it up for the trainer to ride. These helpers often put the horse daily in one of the special "turnout" areas reserved for exercise. Usually the helper was not paid in cash but traded work for free lessons from the trainer. These lessons otherwise would cost about $30 an hour.

Heidi's new helper, Pam, was an exception to the usual rule in helpers. She was not a teenager, but a tiny woman in her early forties.

The first time I saw her, she was standing speaking Spanish with Pablo as he was cleaning out one of the stalls. She had incredibly thick dark brown hair that fell below her waist. I learned later that her dark good looks came from her Mexican heritage.

I also found out that she was the single mother of a teenage girl. She was currently struggling through the local college getting a degree in biology and eventually planning to be a physical therapist. I also found out that she was working for Heidi because she loved horses, but had very limited funds.

She was a high-energy person. I often saw her running to the barn to fetch the next horse for Heidi to school. Unlike most of the teenage helpers who often sulked around with their duties, she was always pleasant and in a good mood. She was definitely an asset to the Ranch.

Scout's rescue from his exile to the pasture came when Pam came to Heidi wanting to take dressage lessons. Heidi did not have any schooling horses unlike Harriett, the hunter-jumper trainer, who owned several ponies and horses that were used daily for lessons. The main reason for this was the difference in the two disciplines: hunter-jumper and dressage.

Dressage horses are so highly trained and sensitive that few owners or trainers would allow anyone, especially a beginner, to ride their horses. The rather sexist joke among dressage riders was "I would lend you my husband before I would lend you my horse."

So, because she had no lesson horses, it occurred to Heidi to let Pam try lessons on Scout. At the beginning level, a highly trained horse wasn't a requirement. The sad fact was that in this case the owner didn't really care about anyone messing up Scout.

The results were incredibly successful. Pam and Scout got along famously. Although she had never had much formal instruction, she was a very competent and seemingly fearless rider. It was heartening to see the big dark horse flying around the ring topped by the tiny lady with hair almost the same color streaming out behind her.

But maybe it was all too good to last. First of all, the weather that winter was the worst in a hundred years. Instead of our usual couple of months of rain, it started to rain heavily at the beginning of November and didn't stop until well into April. The horses in the pasture suffered badly.

Because they were constantly wet, many of them developed a skin condition called "rain rot," which isn't life-threatening but makes the horse look and probably feel terrible. Scout had the worst case of the bunch. He developed bare crusty patches in his dirty shaggy winter coat. Eventually he developed a fever and a bad cough, which caused the vet to recommend that he be taken from the pasture to a dry stall.

The timing could not have been worse to approach his owner to pay $200 more each month to move Scout to an expensive stall. Susan was already a month behind in her payments for the pasture.

I was in the office one Saturday in February when the phone rang.

"This is Susan, Scout's owner," a voice said. "I've just found out that my job is requiring me to move to Guam. I will send money to my boyfriend, Henry, for Scout's past and future board. In the meantime I have made a deal with Pam to try to sell him. She is going to take him out of the pasture and clean him up and show him to potential buyers. She will pay any vet expenses necessary to get him in shape to sell. Whatever profit there is in a sale will be hers."

And so began the best period of Scout's stay at the Ranch.

Pam moved Scout to a stall in the Courtyard full of nice dry cedar shavings. For days he stood with his head hanging listlessly. Everyday Pam gave him the vet-prescribed pills crushed in a pan of hot bran until he began to feel well again.

Then she would take him to the crossties and brush the mud out of his coat and apply the salve to cure the remaining "rain rot." As his thick winter coat was slowly replaced by healthy new hair, Scout started to look like himself again. Finally, every day I would see Pam take Scout into the dressage ring for their lesson. By April, it was hard to tell that he was the same horse that had come out of the pasture in February.

At the same time, Pam was seriously trying to sell Scout because she couldn't afford to pay for his board herself. She paid for an advertisement in *Ride* magazine and often showed him to perspective buyers. It seemed only a matter of time before he would have a new owner.

I was in the office when I got the next set of bad news.

"I don't know what I am going to do about that Scout," Janet said, shaking her head. "I haven't received any money for his board since Susan left for Guam. She owes me more than $1,000 now. I think that boyfriend of hers is just pocketing the money that she sends him. I can't let this go on. I am going to have to confiscate that horse to pay for the debt."

Again I felt that sinking feeling in the pit of my stomach. Since this was a legal if not common practice in the horse world, I was not surprised at her reaction.

"The only problem," I replied, "is that Pam has put a lot of money into him trying to sell him. I know she has spent almost $500 on vet bills and on advertising. And she doesn't have a lot of money to lose."

"I don't have any money to lose either," Janet snapped. "That horse belongs to me now. Tell her I'll give her one more month to sell him."

Before owning the Ranch, Janet had been in the beauty business. She was a striking figure, tall and slim, with her hair cut in a flattering bob. While I was allowing my hair to turn white, hers was always a freshly colored honey shade.

The Ranch was a new venture for her. She was a good businesswoman, especially where money was concerned, but she did not like the management end of the Ranch. She hated dealing with difficult boarder situations. My previous experience in the computer business had cured me of this problem. I had learned how to smile and firmly explain even an unpleasant position in a way that the hearer would understand its inevitability. That made me a very useful employee.

That afternoon I walked up to our big storage trailer where we stored our alfalfa to see if we were running low and needed to order more. The winter had finally ended, and the bare trees were beginning to show outlines of very bright green.

As I passed the crossties, which were used mostly by Heidi's students, I saw that Pam was busy getting Scout ready for a ride.

I could hardly believe that I was looking at the same horse who had come out of the pasture so bedraggled a couple of months earlier. His coat shown from brushing and the expensive feed supplements that Pam had been carrying to him every day in a bucket. As she slipped the bridle over his head, Scout leaned his head affectionately against her side. It was clear that they had become very attached to one another.

"Have you had any luck trying to sell him?" I asked hopefully.

"There is one little girl who takes lessons at Setting Sun Stables who is seriously interested," she beamed, "Anyway, Susan is coming back from Guam next week, and I'm hoping she will get things paid up and straightened out with Janet."

I was away from the Ranch for the next two weeks. My husband John and I drove up the Coast for a weekend at an old inn we visited periodically when we needed to escape. That winter with its constant rain had taken its toll on me. I was tired and needed a rest.

When I returned to the Ranch, I noticed a cryptic note jotted in Janet's handwriting on the huge twenty-inch square calendar lying flat on the desk in the office. It was where we recorded significant events, such as when a horse arrived or left or when we put in orders for alfalfa and shavings. On the square representing the past Wednesday, was written "SUSAN ETON—MEETING!!!!"

I could hardly wait to finish listening to the messages on the phone answering machine so that I could find Pam to learn what had happened. My heart stopped when I heard a message from Janet that said, "Move Odyssey to Scout's paddock."

What had happened to Scout?

I hurried up the dirt road that led from the office to

the area where Scout and most of the Dressage horses lived. I found Pam in Heidi's tack room. She was pouring a delicious mixture of dried ground alfalfa and molasses, a sort of a horse equivalent of Grapenuts, into a big brown plastic garbage can.

"What's up with Scout?" I asked anxiously.

Pam rose up very slowly and looked at me for a few minutes without saying a word. Then her chin began to jerk in a strange way that I could see was an effort not to cry.

"Scout's gone," she blurted out. "Susan gave him to her niece who owns a place near Fresno so she wouldn't run up any more board. She just gave him away without even telling me." Now the tears fell down her cheeks.

I threw my arms around her with an instinct that I had learned when my own sisters were hurting. "Oh, no, you poor thing," was all I could manage to say.

"Janet told Susan she wouldn't give her any more credit and that if she kept running up a bill, she would confiscate Scout. I guess she couldn't take a chance on waiting to sell him. They came to pick him up yesterday. Susan owes me $500 dollars. That's a lot of money for me."

"What happened to the money that she said she was sending to her boyfriend to pay for Scout?" I queried.

"He spent it on his motorcycle. I don't have that kind of money. There was nothing I could do," she cried. "And I'll never see Scout again."

"I'm sure Janet feels bad about it. She is really soft-hearted. There was not much else she could do. She can't run a Ranch on charity," I justified.

"I feel so depressed. I haven't slept for the last two nights."

I struggled to find something positive to say. "Well at least you got Scout in good shape. He was all healthy and happy. Maybe he'll enjoy being out in a pasture again."

"Who knows," she replied, "the niece will probably just sell him now and we'll never know what happened." She turned back to putting the A & M, a packaged mixture of alfalfa and molasses, into the brown can, sniffing loudly.

"When will people learn that horses are not just like a new car that you can buy, try out and then sell when you want with no consequences?" I asked. Now the heavy feeling in my stomach was back again. As I walked back down the dusty road to the office, I wished I had never seen Susan Eton with her red lacquered nails.

Hand-Me-Down-Horses

Hand-me-down-horses are small
They stand in the sun and rest
A hind foot cocked.
They wait for the next little girl
Daring to learn to ride
Willing to take the test.
Hand-me-down-horses are brown
And chestnut and paint and bay
Hand-me-down-horses survive
To teach another day.

Mocha

Every day as I made my rounds about the Ranch in the early morning, I could count on Mocha waiting at his door to be petted. We would visit for a few minutes.

To the uninitiated, Mocha was just a small brown horse. In the pipe paddock where he lived, he was unimpressive next to this neighbor, Victor, a huge black Hanoverian. Most of the other tenants of the Ranch were tall svelte Thoroughbreds or large Warmbloods.

Mocha's friendliness and size were a good hint that his breeding was probably mostly Arabian, although any papers to prove the point had probably never existed or been lost long ago. As I touched his perky concave nose or patted his short sturdy back, I could easily imagine him in a Bedouin tent instead of the muddy little stall.

Mocha was what is known by trainers as a good children's horse, a good first horse on which someone could safely learn the basics of riding: how to start, stop and go over small jumps. Unfortunately I was learning that these trustworthy little first horses were often deserted as the rider grew taller and increased in skill. Usually the owner would eventually want to progress to a larger, more challenging horse, especially one that looked more impressive in the horseshow ring.

I called horses like Mocha "hand-me-down horses."

Ironically, the better a first horse like Mocha did his job in teaching a little girl to ride, the sooner he would be discarded for a new Thoroughbred. Then he would spend months standing idle in his paddock waiting to be bought by another beginner. This was one of those waiting periods for Mocha.

Mocha's present owner was a spoiled little fat girl whom I had never seen riding him. In fact she never came out to the Ranch after having done very poorly in her first show on her flashy new chestnut Thoroughbred. After three minutes in the ring, they both had become so nervous that Harriett, the trainer, had moved them out to prevent sure disaster. The fact is that even Mocha had not been able to teach this child to ride, so he was for sale again—for $5,000.

At that time, this was an unheard of price for such a horse. It was common to pay $10,000 for a Thoroughbred or even $30,000 for a well-trained dressage horse— especially a Dutch or Swedish Warmblood because of their scarcity in this country. A little horse like Mocha usually went for around $500 to $1,000. $2,000 was the most anyone could respectably ask in the current economy. So Mocha was still in his stall every morning hoping to be ridden.

Luckily for Mocha, Harriett was not the type of trainer who sees a horse only in terms of money. She always took care that any horse she worked was well provided for. Mocha was no exception. In this case, Harriett had a friend named Helen who needed a nice little horse to ride, and Mocha was the perfect candidate.

After several rides, Helen and Mocha progressed from

mutual respect to real affection, and Helen become Mocha's sponsor. This meant that she paid for Mocha's board in exchange for being able to ride him at any time.

Sponsoring is a common arrangement in the riding world and is usually beneficial to all parties involved. The sponsor pays for the horse's board so that the owner of the horse saves the monthly boarding money. The sponsor then has a horse to ride anytime without having to put up the cash to buy it or having the responsibility for its future. Best of all, the horse gets ridden. Sponsoring a horse is something like leasing a car instead of buying one.

I had noticed that most riders fall into two categories, those under fifteen and those over fifty years old. It seems that eighty percent of equestrians at boarding facilities are females on both sides of the child-bearing years. This makes perfect sense when you consider how much time and energy a husband and a family take. Many riders have a gap in their careers from age seventeen when they quit riding until sometime in their later years. Suddenly one day they find themselves driving into horse facilities and looking around, wondering why they had forgotten how good horses smell and feel and sound.

Helen was one of these older equestrians at the Ranch. Like other older riders, she found in Mocha something she had felt over 25 years ago and wanted to renew. She offered Mocha's owner $2,500 for him and was immediately refused. They wanted $5,000.

It wouldn't have been so bad if Mocha's owner's parents had been hard up or behind in their mortgage payments. In fact the mother had a substantial amount of money that she had inherited from a well-known local business. But to her, an investment was an investment, even if it was a small bay horse. So the price stayed at $5,000 and Helen went on sponsoring Mocha.

I first heard about the details of the situation about a month after the owners had refused Helen's offer. One day as we were sending out the monthly bills in the office, Janet turned in her desk chair. She straightened out her long elegant legs, shook her head and asked, "Have you heard the awful news about Mocha?"

"No," I faltered.

"Mocha is being put up as a prize in a raffle. That stupid woman who owns him has actually donated him as a prize with a value of $5,000 at a silent auction at that exclusive private school her daughter and several other girls at the Ranch attend."

"What is the point of that?" I countered, "Nobody is going to pay more than a couple of thousand dollars for him."

"Their reason was that if they couldn't get their price for him in a sale, at least they could use him as a loss for a tax deduction!" Janet spit out the last two words as if they left a bad taste in her mouth.

My stomach lurched. I couldn't think of Mocha's soft muzzle and big brown eyes as a tax deduction. It was almost worse than knowing that the highest value of many nice older horses was as meat at seventy cents per pound.

"When is the auction?" I asked.

"Not until school is out in another three months," she sighed.

I couldn't sleep well that night worrying about what might eventually happen to Mocha if he were sold at the auction. Someone could buy him for under $1,000 and make a profit by selling him to be slaughtered.

For the next three months Helen still came out four or

five times a week to ride or groom Mocha. They were inseparable. Mocha's coat and eyes became shiny from all the attention. Everyone watched the pretty woman lead the small bay horse around the Ranch.

As they would pass out of range of hearing, people would look down at the ground and sigh or raise their voices to discuss how terrible it was that Mocha was being auctioned off as a tax deduction. Soon the first question everybody asked as they arrived at the Ranch was if there had been any bids on Mocha.

The answer was that of course Helen had entered a bid and that maybe there was another, but that no one knew for sure. In the office we received notice that Mocha's owners would not require his stall after the date of the raffle.

One Monday I was out in the barn counting the bales of oat hay to see if we had enough to last the rest of the week. I had forgotten that the auction had been held that weekend. I heard shouting coming from the main jumping arena. Instead of the usual slow precise cantering, I saw horses charging in all directions with their riders waving their arms wildly over their heads.

"Helen got Mocha!" I heard over the commotion.

"What happened?" I yelled as I ran over to where Harriett was standing.

Harriett slapped her riding crop against her boot. "They had the auction yesterday. There was only one bid for Mocha. It was Helen's. She had got him for $2,000. Isn't that great?" she beamed.

"I should say so, "I returned. "Isn't that $500 less than she had offered a year earlier?"

"Sure is," she laughed, slapping her thigh in a most

unladylike manner.

I hurried to the office where I immediately filled out a new card to replace the one currently in front of Mocha's stall. I changed the name of the owner to Helen Smith.

Then I put a big red sticker in the shape of a heart after Mocha's name. Sometimes things just work out for the best.

Chief

The voice on the phone sounded desperate, "I haven't slept through the night for three weeks now, and I am losing my mind," she said.

"Who are you?" I asked.

"I rent the pool house up on the hill behind you. Every night at 3:00 AM that brown and white horse in the first paddock starts kicking the pipes and doesn't stop until six or seven o'clock. If you don't do something about it I am going to call the police or the county or somebody."

I knew which horse she was talking about, and the mention of calling the county definitely got my attention.

The brown and white horse had to be Chief. He was a paint Quarter Horse who had been a problem since he had arrived at the Ranch. He was beautiful to look at with huge splashes of white and mahogany. He seemed to have come out of the pages of a book about the Old West. He was the classic Indian Paint.

He was a joy to ride and was gentle with people. His only problem, and it was a big one, was that when he was put away in his stall, he kicked constantly. A couple of months earlier, he had literally knocked in the wooden wall of his first box stall.

So we moved him from that box stall to a pipe paddock. Many horses preferred this open environment to the rather solitary enclosed wooden box stalls. It was like being in a pasture except because of the separating pipes they were unable to move around completely freely. They soon became fond of the horses in the adjacent paddocks. My own horse Shaman loved to stand with his nose next to his neighbor when he dozed.

But not Chief—he continued to kick. Finally he had been moved from one pipe paddock to another in an attempt to find a place where he would be quiet. In spite of this, his back legs were always marred by red cuts and dark bruises.

He never kicked just one foot, but would square off and kick with both hind feet, lifting his powerful rear end into the air. Usually he hit the iron pipes instead of his neighbor who was quick to get out of the way.

Most of us believed that he didn't like other horses close to him, so Heidi proposed the idea that he had been "proud cut." That is when a stallion is gelded and all of its testicles have not completed descended out of the body and so are not completely removed. In effect the horse remains a sort of semi-stallion with many of the stallion's tendencies to fight or bite.

After many moves, I thought we had finally found a place where Chief had run out of horses to fight. The paddock he currently occupied was on the end of the row of ten so there was no horse on his right, and on his left was the oldest, mildest mare on the Ranch whom no stallion in his right mind would interpret as a threat. For the past three weeks since the move, Chief's back legs had been still, and he had seemed content all day. I was surprised at what the tenant of the pool house was telling me.

"Are you sure it was the spotted horse in the first paddock?" I asked.

"Yes," she said. "I went down last night at 4:00 AM, and he was banging on the front rung of his paddock with his left front foot. And he stops at six or so."

I realized that this time Chief was banging away telling the men that it was time for his breakfast which they brought around six.

"Yes and I am going to tell my landlord to call the police or the Health Department if you don't move that horse or do something about it."

Her mention of the Health Department and her landlord definitely made an impression on me. Both had been making our lives miserable for about a year.

I had begun to think of the house on the hill behind the Ranch as a fortress ruled by an evil presence. It was surrounded by an invisible electric fence hidden in the ground and was patrolled by two Rottweilers.

The only contact we had with the owner was his numerous complaints about the Ranch and his reputation with the other neighbors in the lane. He called the dogcatcher to come and get poor old Bo, the Golden Retriever that lived down the street who tended to wander around on harmless visits.

But worst of all, he reported the Ranch to the Health Department for anything that annoyed him. Why he had bought and moved into a house next to an Equestrian Center when he seemed to hate all animals was a mystery to all of us at the Ranch. The rumor was that he was a high-powered lawyer in the City who had moved out to the country for peace and quiet. Obviously, he had been disappointed.

Our first encounter with him was the summer after he had moved in. Like most places with horses, we fought a constant battle with flies when the weather got hot. In spite of all our spraying, they refused to leave the manure pile, which was rather close to our neighbor's property line.

One day as I was in the office, I saw a strange young man who was sneaking around the Ranch. In spite of stylish photographs to the contrary, most horse people dress in rather grubby clothes when they are working every day. I knew this young man was not a patron of the Ranch. He was dressed in spotlessly clean khaki pants and a navy blue gabardine blazer. He had on rather conspicuously new green rubber Wellington boots, as if he were expecting to have to wade through all manner of unspeakable things. He carried a notebook and pencil in his hands.

Eventually, after touring the Ranch, he walked up to the office and introduced himself as our personal representative from the county Health Department. He explained that our neighbor on the hill had complained about the flies and that we would have to do something about them or be subject to a sizable fine. He smiled and said he would return in two weeks to inspect our response.

When I told Janet about the problem, she wanted to avoid a showdown at any cost and decided to move the manure pile away from where it would bother the neighbor. The only place left to put it was right outside the office, so the flies moved in with us instead.

Two weeks later when the young man returned, he approved of our solution, but in walking around the property he found several other things to cite, chief among which were the mosquito larvae in the ditches behind the crossties where the horses were washed. He warned us that the ditches had to be made to drain properly or again we might be fined.

This time Janet had to rent a large backhoe, and Pablo spent an entire hot afternoon re-digging the ditches so that they would drain. For the time being the Health Department was appeased. No one doubted that our neighbor on the hill had been the one to turn us in.

My latest contact with him had been on the morning of the Regional Spring Dressage Show that was taking place at the Ranch. I arrived at six in the morning to oversee the preparation activities. Since we had 96 rides of five to nine minutes each, the first class was to start at 7:30 AM. The court was already decorated with flowers, and someone was testing the public address system with Vivaldi turned up to a deafening pitch. I wasn't surprised when the phone rang as soon as I walked into the office.

An angry voice said, "This is your neighbor on the hill and if you don't stop that music right now, I am going to ruin your show by playing Rap music all day as loud as I possibly can."

Not unsympathetically, I immediately turned the Vivaldi off until it was needed for the first rides.

That had been several months ago. Now Chief, the horse in the outside paddock, was disturbing not only our neighbor, but his tenant. I did not doubt that our lawyer neighbor could cause us trouble if he wanted to do so.

The problem was that the latest move for Chief had been our last resort. At this point every horse owner on the Ranch knew about Chief's habit and refused to have him moved next to her horse because of the possible risk of having it kicked. I didn't know what I could do about the problem.

The solution was suggested by Pablo. "That horse loco . . . maybe he like the pasture."

"Why do you think that would work?" I asked.

"Because in pasture nothing to kick," said Pablo.

"Except the five other horses in the pasture," I replied.

"Maybe they move," said Pablo.

"I think most of them will," I agreed. "But what about Titan? He thinks he is king of the pasture."

After a second warning from the tenant in the pool house, I decided I had no choice. Chief would have to go to the pasture. The next morning Pablo and I took Chief out of his paddock and headed for the pasture. I took with me a long longe whip, of the type used to train a horse while standing on the ground in front of it, to keep the other horses at a distance. Pablo undid the halter around Chief's head and turned him loose.

At first the other horses approached carefully and touched noses with the newcomer. To my surprise nothing happened. Finally Titan came forward very belligerently, snorting and tossing his head. Then Chief did what he had been practicing to do. He wheeled around and started kicking with both back legs.

Instead of running away, Titan mirrored his actions and turned his rump to Chief and kicked back. I almost felt the ground shake as they traded blows for several minutes. It seemed neither of them would quit kicking the other. Chief's white patches began to show bright red streaks of blood.

Finally Titan threw his head up with a rather surprised look and bolted away to stare at Chief from a distance. The battle was over. Chief was the new king of the pasture.

From that time on, Titan never again challenged Chief. Shasta, the little Arabian mare, became Chief's constant worshipful companion, never straying far from his side. And best of all, Chief stopped kicking because the other horses stayed as far from him as he required. The problem was solved.

Later I explained what had happened to Janet.

"What I have been wondering," she mused, "is what that woman is doing renting his pool house in first place. Aside from the Ranch, which is zoned residential\agricultural, this land is zoned for single residences with guest houses. I think that our neighbor is renting out that pool house illegally."

Sure enough she called the county and found that second rental units in that neighborhood were not legal. A couple of weeks later as we were sitting in the office trying to put out the monthly billing on the computer, the phone rang.

"That tractor is waking me up every Saturday and Sunday morning at 7:00 AM when you drag the dressage arena," our neighbor's voice was unpleasant as usual. "If you don't stop it, I am going to call the county and get an injunction against you not to start business before normal hours," he snarled.

This time Janet was ready for him. "Oh, I am sorry," she said. "I guess we are bothering both you and your tenant."

There was a slight pause on the other side of the line. "What tenant?" our testy neighbor asked.

"The illegal tenant you have renting the pool house," Janet replied. "By the way if you are going to call the county, could you please give me the number that you call for complaints?"

"Forget it!" he slammed the phone down.

Now whenever I think about Chief, I remember that both horses and people have to learn to get along with their neighbors.

Pablo

Pablo was one of the best workers we had ever had at the Ranch. He first came to work on a terrible rainy day in January when most of the stalls in the Courtyard were flooding. Janet and I were furiously shoveling wet shavings and straw into the wheelbarrows.

We were doing the work ourselves because our regular worker had quit the night before. With a big grin on his handsome face, Pablo grabbed a pitchfork and told us he would take care of things. In two hours he had done what it would have taken both of us all morning to accomplish.

From then on, Pablo was our right arm. Whenever I asked Pablo to do something, I could count on it getting done as soon as possible. He told me that he had been a jockey in Guadalajara but had been hurt and couldn't ride anymore. His small thin frame did attest to this fact, and often by the time he finished cleaning the stalls, he had a definite limp.

He could do more work in a shorter time than any man we had before. Also his ability to speak English made him a favorite with the trainers who spoke little Spanish.

One of Pablo's best characteristics was his sense of humor. Whenever things went wrong, a smile would lift his straight black Cantinflas moustache, and he would laugh as he went about correcting the problem.

Once when Harriett complained about the fact that the shavings covering the floor in a certain huge Dutch Warmblood's stall were always wet, Pablo explained with a grin, "Is pee too much!"

The problems began when Pablo's girlfriend, Soledad, moved in. When she came to live in the workers' quarters, Pablo's work suffered. You couldn't blame him for being in love with her. She was a gorgeous woman from Columbia. There was real classiness in her light skin and slim figure. Her short curly dark hair was cut in a style that for some reason American women can rarely achieve. My own husband asked who she was with awe the first time he saw her coming out of the small dingy cottage which Pablo shared with Miguel, the other worker.

Pablo tried to get Soledad a job working at the Ranch. At the time we had only two workers. That meant that on two days during the week when each worker had his day off, we would be down to one worker. There were many complaints from the horse owners that the stalls were not being cleaned properly on those days.

Finally, I convinced Janet that it was impossible for one man alone to do all the day's work. This involved feeding sixty horses twice a day and cleaning forty stalls. Also every day very early, it was necessary to drive the tractor pulling a harrow around each ring to smooth the sand evenly for the day's rides. At any time a worker might have to drop what he was doing to quickly handle an emergency that came up, such as fixing a spurting water pipe kicked loose by some horse in its stall.

Another job that required great physical strength was to rescue a cast horse. A horse is said to be cast if it rolls in its stall into a position where it gets stuck with his legs against the wall and is unable to get up. If that occurred, one of the men would loop a rope around the nearest available leg. With brute force he would pull the horse so that it would roll into a position where it could get its feet back under it and stand up again.

Eventually Janet agreed to hire an extra part-time worker for the two days that the regular workers were away.

I had asked Pablo if he knew someone for the job. He suggested Soledad. After getting over the shock of the suggestion, I explained that I didn't think she would be physically able to do the work. Pablo's thin black mustache had dropped so visibly that I reversed myself. I agreed to let her try.

I had been a big advocate for woman's rights in my youth. Besides, I could see where Pablo's logic was carrying him. If Soledad could do the work, maybe eventually she could be the second permanent worker. Then he could share the cottage with her alone instead of with Miguel, the other worker.

So Soledad had started working on Fridays and Sundays. I never knew how she managed to push the heavy wheelbarrows full of hay for the horses' breakfast because that job was done very early, before I arrived at the Ranch at 9:00 AM. Maybe Pablo did all that by himself.

I did see her cleaning stalls looking very chic, even while raking manure. She did a good job. She was finished by noon and disappeared into the house for the rest of the day. I figured that if Pablo wanted to do everything else for her, it was okay with me— just so everything got done somehow.

Everything did get done, and things seemed to be fine for two weeks. Then payday arrived. When Janet made out the paychecks, she paid Soledad half the amount she was paying the men. She explained to Pablo that this was because Soledad was only working half a day and was not available to do the heavy work or drive the tractor.

That was the end of Soledad's work at the Ranch. Pablo told me that she was able to make three times as much cleaning people's houses as she did mucking out horse stalls.

So when the next Friday came, there was a new part-time worker on the Ranch. He was a short stocky older man probably in his late forties with a missing front tooth. He wore a straw hat with a tassel in the back that had surely come with him from Mexico. The fact that he was Miguel's father was evident from the way he ordered the boy around.

In spite of his age, this new man was a great worker. He was able to get twice as much work out of Miguel than we had gotten before. The only problem was that he spoke almost no English. His accent was so different from the Castilian Spanish I had studied that it was difficult for me, or the trainers, to talk with him. This wasn't bad, as he was so smart he was always able to figure out what we needed and do it anyway.

So Hernando, Miguel's father, moved into the workers' cottage. It wasn't long before Soledad moved out into an apartment with friends. The cottage was too crowded for them all. Perhaps too, Soledad was uncomfortable living with the less sophisticated farmer.

That was when Pablo started disappearing. At first it was only a couple of afternoons a week. When I saw him climbing into his old battered white truck, he would claim to be going out for groceries. Eventually he was missing almost every evening. I couldn't find him for the usual emergencies. Hernando had to take his place.

I knew Pablo was visiting Soledad.

Another reason for Pablo' disappearances was that he, Miguel and Hernando were not getting along. I could often hear shouting coming from the workers' house. Pablo once confided in me, "That old man is crazy."

Whenever anything went wrong, each was always blaming the other. Eventually I had to explain twice all instructions regarding a change of feed or which horse to turn out for exercise—once to Pablo and again to Hernando. It was clear that they were not even speaking to each other.

It wasn't long after Soledad left that Hernando approached me with the idea of bringing his family up from Michoxan to live with him in the cottage. He said that he had another son who was a good worker. I relayed the request to Janet whose first reaction was that she didn't think it was a good idea. Besides, where would Pablo live?

One day Hernando came to me and asked me to come with him. I followed him into the cottage. I couldn't believe how dirty and disorganized it was. There were dirty dishes everywhere in the kitchen. When I went into the bedroom, the smell was terrible. The blankets and sheets on the unmade bunk beds looked as if they hadn't been changed in weeks. There were soiled clothes lying everywhere. I guess I shouldn't have expected more from men living together.

With a flourish Hernando pulled back the door to the closet and pointed to a stash of tack neatly piled on the floor. There were two shiny pairs of spurs, a hoof pick, a longe line and several other articles used with horses.

"Pablo take these," Hernando accused.

I defended Pablo, "I am sure they were probably abandoned or thrown away. When Pablo emptied the garbage, he found them."

I could not believe Pablo was a thief. I did believe that Hernando was trying to get Pablo in trouble.

Next Monday as Janet and I were working in the office, there was a knock at the door. I opened it to see Pablo standing there, his eyes flashing with anger. Behind him stood Miguel with his hands in his pockets and Hernando with his eyes averted.

Pablo marched in and took the shabby chair in front of the desk that Mama Kitty had always used as a scratching post. The other two remained standing uncomfortably.

"Miguel banged up my truck," Pablo charged. "He came home drunk last Saturday night."

"It wasn't me," Miguel denied.

"I didn't hear anything," Hernando agreed. "Pablo must have had a wreck." Then he yelled something at Pablo in Spanish.

Janet began to swivel her chair back and forth. I knew how much she hated confrontations, especially when they were conducted in a language she didn't understand. I could tell she felt betrayed by Pablo who had never caused any bother before but who was the instigator of this scene.

"Why are you accusing Miguel of something you can't prove?" She said to Pablo, "Can't you get along with the other workers? I don't want any trouble around here. Now all of you get back to work and don't bother me again with your squabbles."

Pablo looked hurt and shocked as he left the office quickly. He was followed by the other two smirking men.

Frankly, I believed Pablo was telling the truth. After all, someone had done it, and I had seen Miguel come home drunk and belligerent before. Also I had begun to suspect that Hernando and Miguel were trying to chase Pablo off.

If they were, it worked. Eventually Pablo began to disappear even more often. Not only did he miss Soledad, but Hernando and Miguel were making his life at the cottage miserable.

Then an old Thoroughbred died. I was pretty sure it would have happened anyway, even if Pablo had been there to call the vet earlier. After the autopsy the vet said the horse had a huge cancer that had caused a blockage of the intestines.

In any case, it was Pablo' responsibility to check the horses before going to bed at night. He obviously hadn't done it. So he was blamed for the horse's death. This was the final strike against Pablo. He had to go.

So Janet fired Pablo. Pablo again sat in the worn chair across from Janet's desk in the office. His small wiry body slumped to one side. There was a resigned look on his dark smooth face. He looked at me as if hoping I would contradict what Janet had just told him. I could not.

In fact, I had probably decided before Janet that he should be fired, especially when he had started disappearing almost every afternoon. We had all seen this event coming for a long time. The current state of affairs could not be allowed to continue.

Within two months after Pablo left, Hernando moved his family up from Mexico to live in the cottage. What he hadn't told us was that the son who was such a good worker was only twelve years old and that in addition to him there were two other boys, six and eight, and a girl fourteen. We got a few more people than we had expected in the tiny worker's cottage.

One sunny Sunday Hernando invited me into the cottage again. I couldn't believe the transformation. It was spotless. Instead of dirty dishes, the table held a delicious looking meal of tortillas, beans and rice. I could see that the bunks in the bedroom were all neatly made. I was delighted when Hernando's wife invited me to join them for lunch. As we were eating, they suggested that if Janet would buy the paint, they would paint the inside of the cottage.

Every now and then as I looked out the office window, I could see the boys helping Hernando and Miguel pull the wheelbarrows piled with hay. The teenage girl swept the drive and the Courtyard and cleaned the restroom. I could smell a wonderful odor coming from the cottage as Hernando's wife cooked dinner for them all. I guess the old man wasn't so crazy after all.

Still, I miss Pablo, his pencil-thin mustache, his wry smile and his Cantinflas laugh.

Wanda

I had noticed strange tracks in the dirt around the Ranch for some days. They were up and down the main path and wound around in front of the office. They were densest in front of the Courtyard. Wherever there was no pavement, I could see these long forked prints that resembled tracks from some huge bird.

Occasionally I noticed a pile of what had to be excrement. It looked like what pigeons leave on and under statues, but was much bigger and darker. I was not too concerned, as there did not seem to be any damage to the stalls or fences. Also there was no suggestion of it being from a dangerous "varmint" like a coyote or even a fox.

The source of the tracks became evident one morning. I was walking into the entrance to the Courtyard to see if the stalls there had been cleaned properly. Suddenly I was practically knocked down by Smokey the cat streaking out of the enclosure.

Close behind her I saw something that resembled the running dinosaurs in the movie *Jurassic Park*. Only it was much smaller, less than a couple of feet high. It had its long neck snaked out, and its sharp beak pointed right at

Smokey. I jumped aside as Smokey flew by me with the creature close behind.

I almost ran into Harriett as I walked on. I was still turning to look at the rout.

"What was that?" I asked.

"Oh, that is just Wanda," she replied.

"Who or what is Wanda?"

"She is a wild turkey who has settled into the Courtyard. She has made a nest in the tall grass around the crossties where we tack up the horses. She hates cats and makes Smokey's life miserable. Wanda chases her away whenever she sees her."

"Poor Smokey." I thought. "Why is her name Wanda?"

"Because she just wandered in one day," Harriett answered, "Wanda wandered in. Get it?"

I did get it. I recognized then the tracks and excrement I had seen as belonging to a turkey. I had seen the poop before in my own driveway. Like everyone else in the vicinity, I was the victim of an invasion of wild turkeys.

The turkeys had been introduced into the area years earlier as game for sport hunting. Since then they had increased to roam in large flocks. They were a special breed from Mexico, not the usual native turkeys found in the Eastern United States. The males were especially beautiful in the mating season with bright blue wattles on their heads and shining feathers. Wanda was the usual dull brown female.

They had become a real nuisance. At one time I had counted a flock of twenty on my roof. They were especially bad after the nesting season when the new babies hatched. Then they would move in bands of dozens over a prescribed route. My roof happened to be on that route.

The babies were closely guarded by the females. These mothers and nurses who preceded and followed the little ones were on the lookout for predators and other dangers. Wanda looked just like one of those nursemaids, guarding the flock.

"Do you think Wanda can be confused and think the horses in the Courtyard are her flock? She seems to be trying to protect them from Smokey, " I asked Harriett.

"Could be," she said, "or else she thinks she is a horse like they are. It would work out the same way."

As crazy as it seemed, it made sense to me. I had seen a similar thing happen in the field next to my house. A female turkey had deserted the flock to become a member of the herd of goats that lived there. I had seen her grazing with them and disappearing with them into the trees to sleep at night. She was smaller than most of the other female turkeys I had seen and had a limp. At the time, I had decided she was a sort of turkey dropout. If she couldn't keep up with the procession of babies and nursemaids, why not become a goat?

"There is one big problem," Harriet said. "Wanda has been chasing some of the boarders. Some of them are really afraid of her."

"She does look pretty scary when she runs at you with her neck stretched out like that." I thought of the band of Jurassic Park dinosaurs again.

The local turkeys were a problem in more ways than one. A few months earlier there were a series of electrical blackouts on our street. The curious thing was their regularity. Every Saturday morning between 7:00 and 8:00 AM the lights would go out. Then they would come on again in about an hour. It happened four Saturdays in a row.

First the lights would go out. Then in a few minutes I would see the truck from the power company come down the street. Soon afterward, the lights would come on again. I began to wait to get on my computer until after 9:00 when I could predict that the episode would be over.

One Saturday I went out and stopped the truck to talk to the man as he headed back down the street. As usual, everything had been relit.

"It's the darnedest thing," he said, scratching his head. "It was turkeys."

"What?"

"There is a flock of turkeys up on the hill above the powerline poles. The guy who lives there works on Saturday mornings. When he goes out to start his car, he has to shoo them out of his way. Invariably one of the big females flies up and hits the power lines. That causes a short. I have to come by and get them back on again."

"What happens to the turkey?" I asked.

"Electrocuted," he answered.

"Sacrificed," I added, thinking about how strong the urge to protect the flock must be.

"But now that I have figured out what is happening I can fix it."

"We can put spanners on the wires to keep them so far apart that then no flying turkey can contact both wires to cause a short. It should solve the problem."

Sure enough the next Saturday morning and all those thereafter were blackout-free. I forgot about Wanda until a few days later when I was brushing Shaman at the crossties in front of Heidi's office. Harriett walked by leading one of her best jumpers.

"It's a good thing you are doing that here and not in the Courtyard," she said, "Wanda would be after you. She is getting more and more aggressive."

"Maybe she has laid some eggs," I guessed.

"No, I looked," she answered. "No eggs. Maybe she is a frustrated mother." Anyway something has got to be done. One of my smallest pupils refused to go get her horse for a lesson because she had to pass by Wanda."

"Uh oh." I thought, "Turkey soup."

She continued, "I thought perhaps someone might want to shoot her and eat her. But the problem is that it is illegal to fire a gun inside the city limits. Believe it or not, the Ranch is just inside the city limits."

"Wild turkeys don't make very good eating," I countered. "My brother-in-law is a big hunter, and he won't waste time or shot on turkeys. It's cheaper to buy one already cleaned in the supermarket."

"Still," she said, "I told Janet we have to get rid of Wanda. My husband volunteered to catch her and take her out in the woods somewhere far from the Ranch and leave her."

"That would be terrible!" I said. Turkeys are social animals. They need to be in flocks. Can you imagine how awful it would be for poor Wanda to be all alone in the middle of the woods? It would be like putting one of us humans on a desert island."

I couldn't sleep that night worrying about Wanda. From her point of view she was just being a good female turkey. She was protecting the Courtyard from invaders. This included kids as well as cats. She was doing her job as she saw it. It would be unthinkable to punish her for doing a good job as a turkey.

A few days later, Wanda was still there. When I got to the Ranch, I saw her patrolling the Courtyard. Harriett's husband must have been too busy to abduct her.

I was in the office doing the billing on the computer when the door to the office banged open. Harriett came running in with her eyes wide.

"They're coming!' she yelled. "You've got to see this."

I ran to the door and looked out. In front of the office was one of the most impressive scenes I have ever seen. There were three large male turkeys moving in unison along the main road into the Ranch.

It looked like the entrance of the Matador and his entourage into the bullring. A huge gentleman turkey moved at a point ahead. He arched his bright blue neck and gazed disdainfully around him. His beautiful feathers were puffed out to their maximum extent.

Every minute or so, he seemed to rotate on a fixed pedestal a few inches to the left or right. Periodically he would stop and shake his feathers. I could actually hear them rattle as the sun flashed on them showing highlights of russet. As he turned, I had visions of the slow controlled swirl of a Matador's cape.

About a foot behind the leader were two very impressive lieutenants. They progressed slowly in unison, keeping the same distance apart from each other and their chief. Each foot moved exactly in step. Whatever the Matador did, the two following would imitate.

As soon as the leader did anything, immediately the pair behind would echo the same display. When his feathers vibrated, theirs would do the same. The shimmering feathers reminded me of the bullfighters' jeweled suits of light.

Finally, the Matador stopped in front of the office for what seemed like minutes. Then he inched slowly ahead absolutely frozen in his pose. The only movement was one foot at a time moving slowly out and forward. The lieutenants respectfully followed his every move.

I realized that Harriett and I were not the only ones admiring the display. A few feet away at the entrance to the Courtyard was Wanda. With her back turned slightly toward the procession, she was pretending to peck at something on the ground. But instead of being entranced with the scene as Harriett and I were, she seemed to be utterly bored. Only once when the Matador rattled his feathers did she even glance up.

After about thirty minutes of performing, the male entourage turned back toward the entrance gate to the Ranch. Slowly by inches they exited the property.

Then as I watched, I saw something unexpected. Wanda stopped pecking at the ground and looked around. I held my breath. At first she started to turn slowly after the three males. As they moved farther and farther away, she started to follow them. When they exited through the gate and headed back up the road, she began to run.

Since the entourage was moving so slowly, Wanda was forced to suit her pace to theirs. I watched her follow respectfully behind the three males. When they stopped to twirl and rattle their feathers, she would drop back and peck a little at some imagined bug. When they resumed their progress, she would casually but deter-minedly continue up the road a few yards behind them.

Eventually the parade reached the spot where the road passed over the top of the hill. As the males disappeared from sight, I could see Wanda still shadowing the impressive trio. For a moment, I saw her alone at the top of the rise—a small dull brown form silhouetted against the trees. Then she was gone.

"I guess that passes for what you would call riding off into the sunset," Harriett commented with a smile.

That was the last I saw of Wanda. We never saw her again around the Ranch. The empty nest in the Courtyard was deserted. Nobody chased Smokey or scared the younger boarders again. I was very relieved that she had not been kidnapped.

"I guess Wanda decided to be a turkey after all," I concluded.

"She will probably be very happy now," said Harriett.

"But I will miss her." I answered.

Cincinnati

Most of the lady horse owners at the Ranch were either over fifty or under fifteen. There were two real exceptions: Karen and Jane. Many people had trouble telling them apart because they were both in their late twenties with long blond hair, lovely smiles and beautiful thin bodies. They were wonderful riders and good friends.

Even their horses at first glance seemed almost identical. They were both gorgeous bay Arabians in the prime of life. But if you looked closely, you could see that Karen's horse, Cincinnati, had much more white on his feet and legs. The slash of white on his face, a blaze, was also missing on Jane's horse, Jason.

It was thrilling to see the two riders trotting down the trail together, one behind the other. From a distance, they looked like a pair of beautiful twins on a matched pair of horses.

But there the similarities ended. Although they looked very much alike on the outside, the personalities of the two ladies were extremely different. While Jane was cautious and careful, Karen was extremely bold and aggressive. After I got to know them well, it was a mystery to me how they had remained close friends since the second grade.

The histories of the two horses were also very different. I met Karen and Cincinnati first. I was in the office when they first arrived at the Ranch. As always with the arrival of a new horse, things were a little confused.

No matter what time someone plans to deliver a horse in a trailer to a particular destination, something almost always happens to delay matters. Either the truck won't start, the horse refuses to get into the trailer, or traffic and weather prevent an exact estimate of an arrival time.

This time was no different. The first person to arrive at the Ranch was the vet, Dr. Sam Smith, in his shiny white van with Pegasus, the winged horse, painted on the side.

"This girl called and said that she was having a new horse delivered here today and needs a vet check to make sure he is sound before she decides to buy it," he explained.

"What kind of horse is it?" I asked.

"One of those crazy King Farouk horses," he replied giving the name of a famous, popular Arabian breeding stallion.

"See this scar," he said pointing to his forehead. "I got that from one of his colts. They're all crazy. What's more, this one was about to be destroyed because two different owners were not able to handle it. It was sent back to the breeder. Since the horse is ten years old, I guess they just gave up on it as being untrainable. The last owner finally gave it to this old lady who has her own very small horse rescue operation."

We were interrupted by the arrival of a flashy red convertible. I saw Karen for the first time when she stepped out of it. She was stunning.

Almost simultaneously, a long four-horse van drove into the Ranch. A very old lady got down from the truck and opened the back door of the trailer.

A tall bay horse came backing out very fast making a

lot of noise with its hooves on the metal surface of the van floor. With the momentum it had gathered, it started to run around the side of the rig. The tiny lady stepped fearlessly in front of it and grabbed its halter.

The horse, Cincinnati, was gorgeous and obviously sound. He was over fifteen hands tall—a large horse for an Arabian.

He took one look at Dr. Smith and, with the uncanny ability that I have often seen in horses and cats, classified him correctly as a VET and therefore dangerous. Whenever Dr. Smith tried to approach him, he would just back up. It looked as if we were not getting anywhere when Karen walked up to him, took his halter and patted him.

"I won't let him hurt you," she said softly into his ear.

The horse visibly relaxed and stood quietly while the vet checked him out.

From that moment on, in spite of his checkered past, Cincinnati could be classified as one of the calmest horses on the Ranch. He and Karen had bonded instantly. The misunderstood, sensitive horse had only needed someone who was not intimidated by his flashy way of moving and his questionable past. He needed someone who trusted him. He needed someone he could trust. Finally he had found her.

Eventually Karen and Cincinnati began to take dressage lessons with Heidi. Their progress was so fast that after only a few months Heidi decided that they were ready for the first big Arabian horse show of the season.

I was watching Karen and Cincinnati prepare for their first show.

"I have an extra saddle patch for a purebred Arabian," I offered as I walked by the crossties.

"What is that?" Karen asked.

"It has become a big thing now to sew a three-inch rectangle patch on the rear of the saddle pad to show what breed the horse is. Thoroughbreds have a "T" over laid by a "B". Hanoverians have the traditionally shaped "H" of their brand, and Purebred Arabians sport a simple capital "A".

"Will it help?" Karen asked.

"Shaman's patch was very useful early in his show career. He was often the only Arabian competing in dressage shows with the bigger breeds. I was often asked the question 'What breed is that fantastic little horse?'"

"Really?"

"Yes, people were always shocked when I answered 'Arabian.' Common opinion at the time held that Arabians were not capable of serious dressage. They thought only warmblood breeds or other big horses were good at dressage."

"I see."

"Luckily this prejudice has changed now that many Arabians are showing and in fact shining in the dressage arena, just as you and Cincinnati are about to show now."

I felt that it was appropriate for me to give Shaman's extra patch to Karen. Cincinnati was another bay Arabian, although he was much larger than Shaman. I even sewed the patch on the saddle pad since Karen did not know how. Then I wished all three, Karen, Heidi and Cincinnati good luck as they trailered off to the big show.

I heard the show results before the trio ever returned to the Ranch. Later that evening my phone rang with a call from Betsy, the manager of the big show. We had become friends during the years Shaman had attended the same event.

"Well, Heidi has done it again!" she crowed. "And this

time she wasn't even the rider."

"What do you mean?" I asked.

"Not only did Cincinnati and Karen win all their classes," she answered, " they got the award for having the highest point of any horse in any class in the show."

"Pretty good for a first time out," I said trying to sound blasé.

I hurried down to the Ranch to greet their return. I am still convinced that no athletes look more exhausted than horses and riders falling out of a trailer after a long hot day at a horse show. Rising at 4:00 or 5:00 AM to braid the horse's mane and driving from one to four hours in an uncomfortable, bouncy truck pulling a ton of horse is only the beginning. The show itself can include standing all day in the hot sun or freezing rain humoring an excited horse and nervous rider.

The energy required is exhausting. Then there is the long drive home with either the adrenaline rush of winning or the dull depression of losing. The last few miles on the road seem endless. I still have past visions of little Shaman stumbling out of the truck with his head low and staggering behind me to his stall. I don't know who was holding up whom.

In this case the adrenaline was still in control when Karen hopped out of the cab of Heidi's truck. When she saw me she yelled, "We won! You should have seen us. And Cincinnati won a beautiful new blanket for having High Point."

As Cincinnati confidently backed out of the trailer with his head high, I remembered the frightened look he had had the first time I had seen him.

"It's hard to believe this is the same horse," I admitted.

Jason

The relationship of Jason and Jane started very differently from Karen and Cincinnati. When Jane decided that she wanted a horse, she decided to buy a baby. After researching several expensive breeders, she fell in love with the image of a bay colt on a promotion videotape. She paid full price and started training him from scratch.

Jason was about four years old when I first met the pair. Although this is still considered a young horse for an Arabian, Jane had been riding him rather extensively on trails around the county. He had proved very trustworthy under saddle in spite of the fact that he was often a little spoiled and unruly in hand or when being led around. In spite of some rough edges, Jane, although not a professional, had done a good job of training him.

Together they were definitely a good team. And most important of all, they were devoted to each other.

I got personally involved with Jane and Jason because of a problem that is common to many horses. Many horses have bad associations with a horse trailer. They are like a cat that associates the cat carrier with going to the vet and therefore runs and hides the minute that box appears. Aside from the fact that no one would like to be shut in a box that rocks and bounces along at fifty miles an hour, horses often associate that box with leaving their families and friends to go to a strange new place.

Jason was terrified of any horse trailer. When led up to one, he would fall back on his haunches, spin around pulling the lead rope out of Jane's hand, and run away. Since no one can hold onto a half ton of running horse, Jane was losing the battles.

Jane approached me early one morning as I was walking around checking the stalls in the Courtyard.

"How did you get Shaman to go into a trailer so easily?" she asked.

"When he was only a colt, a few months old, my friend Katherine, who first owned him, taught him," I answered.

"How?"

"She put his mother in one side and put some tasty food in the front of his side. After a couple of times he didn't even care when the box started moving. He thought it was his own personal gourmet restaurant."

"Let's try it," she proposed.

So Jane and I got Jason over his fear of the trailer by putting Shaman in first and then bribing Jason with grain to follow. It worked. Soon he would enter the box on the first try.

In the process, Jane and I started riding trails together. We would drive the trailer to a nearby trail, take the horses out, and ride a couple of hours.

This was great for me because it was the reason I had bought Shaman in the first place. Jane was very understanding of the fact that at my age of sixty years, I wanted Shaman to walk quietly instead of charging along like a teenager. She always had Jason in perfect control even on the steepest hills or scariest woods.

Eventually I even let Jane drive the truck so that she could learn how to handle a rig. Our relationship was mutually beneficial. She and Jason learned to trailer, and Shaman and I got to go on nice long trail rides.

On one of our trail excursions, Jane confided to me that she was thinking of moving Jason away to another Ranch. It seemed that she and Karen were not getting along very well. The main reason was that Karen and Heidi were becoming closer when attending their horse shows, and in the process were leaving Jane out of things. In effect it was the old situation of "two's company; three's a crowd."

It was further complicated by the fact that Heidi was Jason's trainer as well as Cincinnati's. Jane felt that Heidi was unfairly favoring Cincinnati. I attempted to smooth things over by explaining that Heidi was a very focused person. Whenever she decided to show a horse as she was doing with Cincinnati, she did it all the way, no holds barred.

I tried to get Jane not to take things personally, but to see things as just the way the horse show world worked. I told her that Heidi had done the same when she was concentrating on Shaman and that this had upset the owner of another horse, Salem, that she was also training. This extreme concentration was Heidi's weakness as well as her greatest strength.

"You know what I have a good mind to do," Jane said. "I think I'll put Jason in the show too."

"Why not?" I agreed, although I really didn't think that she and Jason were ready for the show ring yet.

So Jane and Jason starting working on their dressage basics in the arena. Jason was in good physical shape from all their trail riding. Because of Jane's hard won control over him, they progressed very well indeed. When the next big Arabian show rolled around, Jane entered Jason along with Karen and Cincinnati.

My involvement was largely clerical. I had learned the hard way with Shaman to which organizations you had to belong and which applications had to be submitted to whom by which date. I helped Jane with the paperwork to make sure that her horse was registered in her name and entered in the show on time.

In fact the show that was coming up was one in which I was personally involved. It would be held near the Ranch by an organization that was promoting the Arabian horse as a versatile sport horse instead of a brainless beauty. I was one of the charter members.

I was even scheduled to "work the gate." This literally meant standing between the warm-up arena where the prospective competitors careened around and the entrance gate to the show arena. My job was to check the large numbers pinned on the side of horses' bridles to make sure that they entered the arena at the exact time they were scheduled to ride. I loved the job because I could see the horses up close and meet the riders personally.

I was definitely worried by the time I saw Heidi's rig containing Cincinnati and Jason arrive. The other competitors for the Training Level class that Karen and Jane were about to enter were already in the warm-up arena. They were an impressive lot.

Most of the riders were professional trainers like Heidi. Also there were more of the big horses that were half-Arabian and half-Warmblood that made such an impressive appearance in the ring. These horses had been winning many of the shows lately. Several of the horses were even stallions with lots of style and sexual energy. I was definitely worried for my friends.

Jason was scheduled to ride next to last. Then Cincinnati was the very last horse in the class. But as the show progressed and I ushered one horse after the other into the dressage arena, I became less and less concerned. The big Half-Arabs seemed to be beginners with very little training, and most of the stallions lowered their scores by misbehaving at some point during their rides.

Eventually it was time for Jason and Jane to enter the ring. Luckily Jason behaved beautifully. They had an almost perfect ride. It was clearly the best ride yet. Since Jason was the least trained horse and this was his first show, I figured he had secured a clear second place behind Cincinnati, whom I now expected to be the winner of the class.

However, from the minute Cincinnati entered the arena, I knew something was wrong. He kept looking outside the arena instead of concentrating on his test. When he passed where Jason was standing at the entrance to the arena, he jerked his head up and whinnied at him. This was a definite fault. His final score placed him fourth instead of first in the class.

Jason and Jane had won. But in the process, they had defeated their best friends and upset the planned order of things.

About an hour later, I looked over to the parking lot where the trailers were parked. I saw Heidi and the girls loading up their horses. Obviously they were not going to stay for their second rides later in the day. I was a little worried about what might have happened.

Shaman and I did not go trail riding with Jason and Jane for the next few months. It was the time of year for Shaman to take his three-month annual vacation back in the pasture where he had been born. He got to be just a horse for a couple of months. And I got a chance to sleep late or do some traveling.

After a three months' absence, when I finally arrived back at the Ranch, I was apprehensive about what had happened between Karen and Jane. I shouldn't have worried.

The first thing I saw was the two girls chatting happily together while washing their horses. Cincinnati and Jason were standing dripping side by side in the crossties. The ladies both turned and greeted me happily as I approached.

"What's going on?" I asked as casually as possible.

"We're getting Cincinnati ready for a show," Jane responded. "So far he has the highest median score of any horse for the prize given by the local Arabian associations. Even if he doesn't do well tomorrow, he has it in the bag, because he can still drop the lowest score from our calculation."

"Is Jason showing, too?" I hesitated.

"No, he and I would rather stick to the trails," Jane said. "I am just helping Karen get Cincinnati ready. He is much quieter if Jason gets a bath along with him."

As I walked away, I figured that the two of them had worked things out again the same way they had done since they had first met in the second grade.

Whether they are horses or people, good friends can usually work things out.

Smokey

The long white stock trailer rolled very slowly in front of the office with its tires making a crunching sound on the gravel. It was empty. The dark open area at horse eye level all around under the green top contrasted with the shining spotless sides of the vehicle. Soon it would reveal the faces of the first four of Harriet's horses to leave the Ranch.

"Well, I guess it is really going to happen," I said to Janet who was sitting at the desk avoiding looking out the window.

"Harriet is so stupid," Janet said. "We'll be better off without her, even if we can't pay the mortgage this month. She has been a great hunter-jumper trainer for us for years. But if she isn't happy with the way we do things, she should take all her horses and leave. There are plenty of other trainers in this area."

She still refused to look out the window as the trailer stopped.

There was a group of people standing in the entrance to the Courtyard where the more expensive of the hunter-jumper horses were kept. Not far away were parked several Mercedes, BMWs and the odd Lexus. I saw the faces of the fathers of many of our teenage boarders. I had seen most of them only once before when they had signed the Boarding Agreements and handed me large checks for the first and last months' rent of their horses' stalls.

I had talked to many of these fathers on the phone when they had called mostly to make complaints about stalls that they did not consider clean enough or to report leaks in the roof, both real and imagined. They were in a rather festive mood at the moment, bantering with each other and trying not to look concerned as their daughters scampered around gathering up tack and equipment.

Two large expensive Dutch Warmbloods stood waiting nervously. Their heads were high with excitement as they pulled on the lead ropes in their small owners' hands.

"None of this would have happened," Janet complained, "if she had just paid us what she owed us."

"I never will understand how she could go back on your contract and not pay you the standard ten percent of all her training fees. She must have been making a fortune with over twenty horses at $300 a month."

"That is just the problem," she explained, "We never could get her to actually sign the contract. And not only that, we didn't have any proof of how much she was actually making."

"Also I guess she never got back ahead of the game after her bankruptcy at her own stable two years ago," I said, trying to be generous.

In spite of all I knew about the situation, it was hard not be taken in by all of Harriett's tales of woe.

"She had enough money to buy that fine new four-horse trailer and truck. I bet it cost at least $60,000," observed Janet.

"She was trying to set her new husband up in the horse hauling business after he lost his job," I explained, "But I agree that she owed you her ring fees first."

As I spoke, I watched Harriett's new husband climb down from the cab of the horse van he had exchanged for his big black Harley. His curly red hair, bushy beard and handle bar mustache seemed out of place among the well-styled and sprayed cuts of the boarders' fathers. His white tee shirt and faded jeans contrasted with the Brooks Brothers shirts and pants and Topsiders of most of the waiting group.

"My problem is that Burt doesn't know a thing about horses. I wouldn't let him touch Shaman, much less load him in a van," I said, shaking my head. It always amazed me when I saw someone set himself up as an expert on something when others know better.

"Yes, but they know even less," Janet said, nodding her head at the assembled fathers.

That was one of the facts of the horse world. There were two types of horse owners. One was the type who spent as much time with their horses as possible, for whom no task was too menial, from picking hooves to shoveling manure. A friend of mine had even brought out a sleeping bag to spend several nights in front of the stall where her big dressage horse was sick with a disease not unlike strep throat, called Strangles. Most of us older lady owners fell into this category.

The second type was the owner who only saw their horses when they rode once or twice a week. They expected their trainer to handle all the everyday dirty work for which, of course, she was very well paid. Most of Harriett's clients fell into this second category, especially because most of them were still in school during the week. The actual owners were their fathers, who had neither the knowledge nor the desire to be more involved. The whole system was based on complete confidence in the fact that everything the trainer said was above question. This wasn't hard to perpetuate as long as the ones who paid the bills remained ignorant, and not too many horses went lame or became bad-tempered from ill treatment.

In the case of Harriett, for the most part she earned her money by taking good care of the horses in her charge. She was always available at any hour of the night or day if a horse coliced. I believed that she genuinely cared about each of them. The fact that her methods were rather rough compared to Heidi's didn't mean she wasn't a good trainer.

Most of the trainers in the hunter-jumper world were traditionally rather heavy-handed. Maybe the aggressive horses they worked with responded best to that type of treatment. A horse that would charge a five-foot fence at full tilt with someone hanging on its mouth wasn't necessarily the most delicate creature in the world. Unlike the dressage horses that responded to the slightest pressure of a leg against their sides, it often seemed to take a whip to get results from some of these old Thoroughbreds. I was not sure whether they started out that way or ended up that way after years of conditioning.

As Burt led the first horses toward the trailer, I saw a flash of gray fur through the long legs.

"Smokey is really upset by all of this," I observed to Janet.

Smokey, the slim female cat with very short gray fur, was the least tame of all the cats on the Ranch. I often saw her sleeping in the sun on a horse blanket that had been left out on someone's tack trunk. Sometimes she would let me touch her, but most often she would stretch, jump to the ground, and stand looking at me from a short distance away. I had the feeling that she probably had a pretty good reason for not trusting people very much.

But if Smokey didn't trust people, she loved horses. She would often stand in the door of a stall and allow its resident to reach its head way down to touch her with his big horse nose. Then she would arch her back to rub and allow her thin tail to run along her friend's big face. I often wondered if at night, when everyone had gone home, she hopped up on some broad equine back to sleep.

"She had better not take that cat with her," Janet answered, looking up belligerently for the first time. "That cat belongs to this Ranch."

"But Harriett has been the one to feed her all along," I responded.

"I don't care, "Janet said. "He was at the Ranch before she even got here."

I knew Janet cared a lot about the Ranch's cats. She always bought cat food even when she was having a cash-short month. But Smokey was not on my list to feed, as were Abner, Mama Kitty and Casey who lived in the barn. Smokey had been fed by Harriett, who was very attached to her.

"Smokey knows that her world is changing and is upset," I answered. "She is going to miss all her horses."

I watched as Burt took the lead rope and led the first horse into the twenty-foot long van. He positioned her at a slight angle crosswise, her head facing the left side and her tail to the right. Although she went obediently, I could tell she was frightened from the way she immediately began to call to anyone who would listen. Burt fastened the iron gate that would partition her from the next horse tight against her side.

Harriett's school horses, who were used to being trailered, went in quickly and quietly. The group around the van cheered as these two horses cooperated with the proceeding.

The fourth and last horse to fill this load was led up by one of the girls. It was Louie, a huge, rather green four-year-old Dutch Warmblood, for whom her father had just paid over $30,000. In spite of and perhaps because of his audience, this horse took one look at the trailer full of the three other horses and planted his huge feet firmly on the ground. He refused to get in.

The roar of laughter that issued from the crowd had two results. It strengthened the gelding's resolve never to enter "THAT THING" and caused a flush of embarrassment to spread over the face of the owning father. In an attempt to save the situation, the man picked up a nearby broom and started to hit the poor frightened horse on the rear end.

Of course this had the opposite of the desired result. The frightened young horse backed quickly and dangerously away from the gaping trailer into the crowd of expensive shirts and creased khaki pants. He almost stepped on Smokey who scampered out of the way as oxford cloth shirts and creased khaki pants scattered in all directions.

No amount of pulling on the lead rope by Burt or coaxing by the broom could get that horse to enter the trailer.

"That's the way to teach a horse how to hate a trailer." I said to Janet.

I thought about how Shaman now almost always walked quickly into Heidi's trailer. The first time we had taken Shaman to a show had been different. It had taken us almost half an hour to coax him into that scary box. But Heidi had never raised her voice and kept constant pressure on the lead rope until Shaman had finally consented to follow her into the trailer.

Harriett's new trailer, with another horse instead of Louie, pulled back past the office window to leave the Ranch. Four pairs of frightened eyes now filled the open space under the green roof.

"Let's see, with twenty horses that will be the first of five loads. The new place where they are going should take about an hour round trip. That should take up the rest of the day," Janet calculated.

"I don't think I can take much more of this. I am really going to miss some of these kids and most of the horses. I think I'll go on home if you are going to be here," I said to the top of Janet's head.

When I arrived the next morning, the Ranch was eerily quiet. With almost half the horses gone and no teenagers cowboying around in the jumping arena, it didn't seem like Sunday morning at all.

As I walked around the empty Courtyard, I saw something that disturbed me. Lucia, a gray Thoroughbred mare, the only horse left in the now deserted row of stalls on one side was beside herself with fear at being left alone. She was drenched in sweat as she paced back and forth calling to her departed neighbors. I had a hard time controlling her as I moved her into the barn, which was still full of horses. She calmed down immediately as soon as she was in the new stall with her head sticking out into the aisle with the others.

When I returned to the Courtyard, I felt something soft against my leg. I looked down to see Smokey's yellow eyes looking up at me. I realized she had not been fed since Harriett had left yesterday, so I got an extra can of cat food out for her when I fed Mama Kitty and the others.

Although she had never been very friendly to me before, this morning Smokey was my shadow. She followed me closely as I made my rounds of the Ranch checking on all the horses.

It wasn't long before I saw Harriett's red Bronco pull into the parking lot. When Harriett got out, I saw she was carrying one of those cardboard pet carriers that they give you at the veterinarian's office.

"I guess you've come for Smokey," I volunteered. "You know Janet doesn't want you to take her."

Smokey came running from the porch of the office to where Harriett was standing and rubbed rapturously against her legs.

Harriett looked me straight in the eye. "One thing I know about you," she said, as she picked Smokey up and put her into the carrier. "You like cats even more than you like horses, and that's saying a lot."

"I guess a cat thief is not as bad as a horse thief," I conceded. "She isn't going to be happy here without you and all her horses."

"It's always been my idea that the person who feeds a cat owns it." Harriett smiled as she carried the now heavy box toward the Bronco.

As I watched the Bronco drive away, I hoped that Janet would think Smokey wandered off on her own.

Cats do that sometimes.

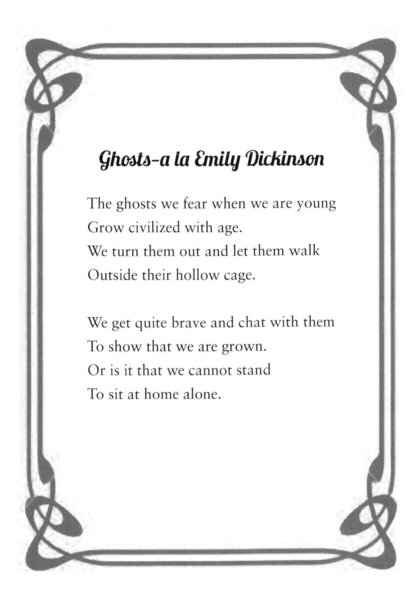

Ghosts-a la Emily Dickinson

The ghosts we fear when we are young
Grow civilized with age.
We turn them out and let them walk
Outside their hollow cage.

We get quite brave and chat with them
To show that we are grown.
Or is it that we cannot stand
To sit at home alone.

♘

Dr. Stern

I first met Dr. Stern long before Shaman was born. I was going for a trail ride with Katherine, the owner of Shaman's mother, at the national park near Shaman's birthplace. Our horse trailer held Sheriff, the steady chestnut gelding I would ride, and Shaman's gorgeous bay mother, Shamina, for Katherine.

We both loved the secondhand rig that Katherine's father had bought. I felt real affection for the old Ford truck that pulled the rusty horse trailer. It saved us from having to ride to the trailhead down the narrow coastal road, dodging tourist cars and the occasional produce truck. Every time I saw the logo of the Arabian Horse Association on the driver's side door, I breathed a sigh of relief. It saved me a heart-stopping twenty minutes of holding my breath riding down the uneven side of the road, praying that no dog would come running out to scare the horse into oncoming traffic.

We pulled into the parking lot at the trailhead, climbed down out of the truck and walked around to the back to unload the horses. As usual, we had heard a lot of bumping and banging coming from the trailer while we were driving. For some reason Sheriff had trouble keeping his balance in the swaying vehicle.

We lifted up the stiff bars that held the heavy back gate in place and lowered it to make a ramp. Then we undid the butt-chains and gave a little pull on the horses' tails to signal them to back out of the trailer.

Sheriff stepped out. I could see that he had hurt himself again. There was blood on the white sock on his left hind foot. We bent over to examine the damage.

"I know an easy way to solve that problem," said a man's voice behind us.

We straightened up to see a handsome, grey-haired gentleman. He was not much taller than we were, and he exuded a positive, cheerful energy and authority. His trim body was dressed in riding clothes, and his feet were shod in well-worn riding boots. He obviously spent a lot of time around horses.

"Really, how?" I answered. " I'm afraid I am going to have to buy some leg wraps."

"No," he said. "Just get rid of that center divider between the horses in the trailer. It will lift right out."

"How can that help?" Katherine asked.

"The two horses will just lean on each other for balance. Then he won't slip around," he said.

Katherine and I looked at each other skeptically.

He laughed, "I don't know why they put those divider things in there. I think they were invented by the devil."

As he walked back to where his horse was tied, we began to saddle up Sheriff and Shamina.

"Who was that masked man?" I asked, echoing the old Lone Ranger television program.

"That was Doctor Stern," Katherine answered, looking very impressed. "He is one of the most respected veterinarians in the area. Mother and I attended a class on horse medicine that he taught for the community college. He was an aviator in World War II."

"He sure seemed nice and friendly," I replied.

"Not only that, he's one hell of a trail rider. They say he can ride for hours and over anything. He's a big endurance rider. He's the oldest rider to ever complete the Travis Cup."

"Just what is that exactly? I've heard people talk about it," I answered.

"It's a one hundred mile ride down this side of the Sierras," she explained. "The average time to finish is a little less than eleven hours. Men, women, and young people compete together."

"Wow! What kind of horse can do that?"

"It's often been an Arabian. They have vet checks at many spots to check the horse's condition and eliminate any who are in distress. That's why only a little over half of the riders finish."

"I couldn't even think about doing that," I replied. " A four-hour ride over these hills is enough for me. If we weren't so happy with our current vet, I would certainly use him."

The next weekend when we headed for our trail ride, we found out that Dr. Stern was absolutely right about the center divider in the trailer. Before we left Katherine's ranch, we pulled it out from between Sheriff and Shamina. All the way to the trailhead there were no banging noises from the trailer. When we opened the back door, we could see two round horse behinds leaning on each other. There was no blood on Sheriff's legs as he backed out of the trailer. Dr. Stern was absolutely right!

Several years later, when I moved Shaman to the Ranch and had to choose a new vet, I chose Dr. Stern. I even recommended him to newcomers to the Ranch. But he was soon replaced by his son Richard, who was taking over much of his work. They became known as Young Dr. Stern and Old Dr. Stern.

Young Dr. Richard Stern really understood horses. Shaman loved him! He must have gotten his ability to work with Arabian geldings from his father. Instead of being put off by their energetic and dramatic reactions to things, he appreciated their honesty and spirit.

If anyone asked, I explained Shaman's wide-eyed snorts by saying, "Shaman has opinions."

Old Dr. Stern may have cut down on his vet calls, but he did not cut out his trail riding. He often joined Herman, another World War II veteran, at the Ranch.

Herman had been in the Navy during that war, and like Old Dr. Stern he was still riding. He went out alone on the trail several times a week on his small grey Arabian mare. I would see him loading her into his own old trailer to head out to the best long trails. Occasionally he and Old Dr. Stern would meet and ride together. It was impressive that they were still riding, even though both were in their eighties.

I was one of the first people to hear about Old Dr. Stern's death. Shaman had an appointment for some of his annual shots. I was putting on my old barn clothes to go out when the phone rang.

"Young Dr. Richard will have to cancel your appointment today," said a shaky voice. There was no more explanation.

"Is something the matter?" I asked, since a cancellation

like this was quite unusual. There were other vets at the practice who could fill in if needed.

After a pause, the receptionist answered, "His father, Old Dr. Stern, has died. They found him slumped over his desk this morning."

"I can't believe it," I gasped, "He went on a trail ride with Herman a few weeks ago."

"I know," the voice answered. " He completed a nineteen-mile long distance relay a couple of months ago. But he is gone."

I knew he would be missed. I had recommended him as a vet to many people at the Ranch. Everyone would miss his good sense of humor and calm demeanor.

It wasn't long before I heard from Joan, one of my horse friends. "There is going to be a memorial service for Dr. Stern next Thursday," she told me on the phone. "It is going to be at one of his patients' big barns near his practice. It was announced in the newspaper. Everyone is invited. Let's go together. I'll pick you up."

"Okay," I answered.

On the day of the service Joan drove her car to the chosen location. It was hard to find as it was hidden way back in horse country. On the way we made a couple of wrong turns and got lost. It was before she had gotten a smart phone with a GPS system. A tangle of little lanes and roads finally led us to the place.

It was a huge white barn in pristine condition. In front and on both sides was a large parking lot. It was packed.

"There must be sixty cars here," she said. "Where am I going to park?"

"It looks like you're going to have to go back to the road and find a place there," I answered. "It's lucky that we didn't wear fancy shoes."

Eventually we were able to find a spot about fifty yards down the road. When we reached the entrance to the property, we realized that our rough walk was over. Several golf carts were taking guests from the parking area to a spot some distance away on the top of a hill. We hitched a ride on one of them.

On the knoll was a lovely meadow surrounded by trees. More than a hundred people were seated on thick green grass, unusual for a horse barn. We took our places.

It was quiet, but not depressing. People of all types were chatting and smiling at each other. We sat next to some people dressed in work clothes speaking quietly in Spanish—apparently barn workers. They made room for us with a friendly smile.

Other guests were obviously wealthy horse owners in expensive Eastern riding clothes. Some ladies had on light-colored sundresses to accommodate the August weather.

The common denominator was hats. Almost no one there was without one. The styles ranged from worn straw cowboy hats to floppy southern belle numbers. None of them looked new. I wore my own old straw western hat with the hawk, buzzard and owl feathers I had found on the trail stuck in the headband. Most of the hats had chinstraps to keep them from blowing off at a gallop.

This was clearly a group of those who spent many hours outdoors in all sorts of weather. These were horse people.

Suddenly we heard a trumpet playing Taps. The mournful notes were coming from the road that wound up the hill behind the seated group. It was accompanied by the sound of hooves of several horses slowly growing louder and louder.

We all turned at once to see the funeral cortege. There were four pairs of riders moving at a slow walk toward us. It was the mounted police from the city. As they passed in front of us, we saw their uniforms and shiny riding boots up close. Their horses were not flashy, but steady dark ones with their heads bowed.

At the end of the line was Wesob, Dr. Stern's Arabian gelding. The saddle on his back was empty. In the stirrups were a pair of worn boots turned backwards. It was the "Riderless Horse," a reminder of JFK's funeral almost exactly fifty years earlier.

"Dr. Stern was the vet for the city mounted police for years," Joan whispered. "I guess they wanted to honor him."

I could hear a lot of sniffling around me. My own eyes filled with tears. Luckily I found an old piece of tissue in the pocket of my pants. I blotted my face as unobtrusively as I could.

Members of Dr. Stern's large family were gathered together, facing the crowd. They were all wearing identical T-shirts saying STERN FAMILY MEMBER.

Young Dr. Stern walked to the front of the group as the last of the mounted guard passed by. Moving tributes to the old vet followed. Friends and family told about his youth and dedicated life as a veterinarian. An old riding buddy described his later exploits on horseback. Someone played a Mozart clarinet piece, and another read poetry. I heard later that the entire occasion had been planned and described in detail on paper years ago by Old Dr. Stern himself.

When the service was over, we were directed to move down the hill to the barn. The crowd of people walked quietly down the gravel road. The reverence and dignity of the group reminded me of processions I had seen of professors at famous old English colleges. A few people chatted in hushed voices. Others smiled sympathetically at each other. Most of the old hats were tilted downward in contemplation.

As we left the funeral service, everyone was given a parting gift to remember the occasion: our choice of a plant from a large collection of various succulents set up at the exit. Dr. Stern had wanted to give each person something living by which to remember him. Succulents were considered appropriate because they were tough and needed little care. Each person walked out to his car with a small pot of a growing plant in his hand. Joan still has hers growing in her garden.

After a few minutes we walked through a screen of trees into a large sunny garden. Suddenly we found our sadness interrupted by a live band playing Country & Western music. Immediately the mood changed to one of celebration. People were smiling and chatting as they encountered riding buddies they had not seen for years.

There were several large tables at various spots on the thick green grass. Three were bars manned by white-coated bartenders. One bar offered only soft drinks, beer and wine, but two were well-stocked with many bottles of the best liquor available.

I found two large tables covered by huge plates of food. One wooden bowl as big as a saddle was full of guacamole. Another platter as big as a folded saddle blanket held wedges of several different cheeses.

As I headed for the guacamole and chips, I was stopped by a waiter with a tray of hot hors d'oeuvres. I took a toothpick of something delicious wrapped in bacon.

When I finally reached the sea of mashed avocado, I saw an old cowboy I had seen often on the trail.

"Have you ever seen anything like this?" he asked, holding his slightly green fingers delicately to the side of his face.

"Never," I answered. "Of all the expensive catered wedding receptions and business conferences in all the big cities and fancy resorts, I have never been to anything quite like this."

"It's a shame Dr. Stern had to miss it, isn't it?" he grinned.

"You're right," I replied, "and I never thought I would say this."

"Say what?" he asked.

"That the best party I ever attended was a funeral."

Epilogue: Twenty Years later

I am enjoying my most favorite activity in the world, shedding out Shaman. His soft velvety winter coat is coming out in soft, itchy clumps as I pass the stiff metal curry comb over his solid body. It is a bright spring morning, and we are standing in the pasture as he grazes. The puffs of hair blow away from the tool onto the new grass. I like to think that some bird will come find them and take them away to cushion its nest. If nothing else, doing the job out here keeps from littering the floor of Shaman's stall.

I am happy to see that this will be another year without the dreaded Cushing's disease, a hormonal condition that sometimes causes old horses to become shaggy as Yaks. Again this year, Shaman's coat is emerging with its original shiny reddish brown glory. He seems to be enjoying being brushed and only kicks at his belly occasionally when a clump of fur blows off my curry comb and tickles.

Shaman has weathered the past twelve years better than I. Even knowledgeable horse people are amazed when I tell them that he is 28 years old. It doesn't surprise me as he comes from long-lived stock. His grandfather,

Khemosabi, lived to be 33 and his mother died just last year at 37.

The truth is that he hasn't worked very hard in the last few years. His show career ended fifteen years ago. I had to quit riding five years ago because of my foot. I broke it kicking off a garden clog, and it still hurts if I try to put pressure on it. If I ride for any time at all, the pressure of the iron stirrup makes me limp for days.

I don't really mind not riding anymore. At my best I was only an occasional trail rider. My favorite horse activity has always been grooming and just being close to Shaman. Luckily I had Heidi to take advantage of Shaman's superb gaits and show potential. I remind myself that the owners of the horses that compete in the Kentucky Derby don't ride the horses themselves, but rely on professional jockeys.

Shaman has not been idle in the past twenty years. Like the famous ballet stars of the past, he has gone from performing to teaching others. His most successful student was Alice, a very talented and determined young lady who now shows her own horse and has won her Silver Medal for dressage. Shaman taught her the necessary figures and movements, the half pass, the turns on the haunches and forehand, and the flashy final halt at the end of a test.

But he hasn't only taught the aspiring dressage competitor. A month ago he participated in a 4-H clinic of little girls from six to eight years old. He stood as still as a heron while they reached up to brush him. He held his head down quietly for a blonde little girl to learn to put on his halter. Then he walked very slowly as one child at a time led him up and down the path in front of the office. If anyone could have seen him tearing around the pasture an hour earlier, they would not have believed they were looking at the same horse.

When Shaman is not grazing in the pasture or being ridden, he is in his pipe paddock next to D.J., the love of his life. She is another beautiful bay Arabian, but she is a mare of a different body type. She is much bigger than Shaman. Seeing them together reminds me of Cyd Charisse and Gene Kelly. They have been living in adjacent stalls for almost fifteen years now, and one never fails to whiny when the other leaves.

Every morning at 8:00 AM my husband, D. J.'s owner or I turn the two out together in the pasture at the front of the Ranch for the morning. When it is my turn to put them out, it is the best part of my day. Even though I am now 73 years old, I feel as young as when I first saw Shaman at his mother's side over twenty years ago.

I have had several birthday parties for Shaman, one when he was ten years old and another when he was twenty. The last was when Shaman's 25th birthday coincided with my husband's 75th. My calculation that together they would be one hundred years old, a full century, couldn't be ignored. John made wonderful invitations on the computer with pictures of both of them. We sent them to our friends inviting them to a "One Hundred Year Birthday Party" at the picnic area of the Ranch.

I engaged a friend, a professional classical guitarist, to play. We bought cases of champagne, fancy party tablecloths for the rickety picnic tables, and ordered a cake. Of course it was a carrot cake. It was a wonderful party in spite of the fact the June date was so hot that the icing on the cake melted. Thank heavens the apple and old fig trees on the lawn gave us some shade. Many of the guests brought carrots and apples for Shaman. I was really delighted that Heidi was able to make it, although she now has a dressage training facility of her own. Alas, Foster, the dog, is no longer with us, but Heidi's ten-year-old son made a suitable replacement.

As I curry away Shaman's old winter hair with one hand, I feel his silky new coat with the other. His muscles are solid and warm under my palm. Someone once said that there was something about the outside of a horse that was good for the inside of a man. I know that somewhere in my genes this action is natural to me. I think about all my ancestors who did this before me, those whose very lives and fortunes depended on the same bond that exists between Shaman and me.

I think of my great-grandfather who was a Captain in the Civil War. He was wounded in one of the last big battles. When he returned home, he found that his favorite, fine mare had been taken from his farm by the opposing troops. He stayed home with his wife and small children just long enough to recover from his wound. Then he disappeared for over a year. When he returned, he was leading his horse. Until the day he died, he never told anyone how or where he got her back. I think that I am glad he didn't tell all the details. I don't believe I really want to know them. I would probably have done the same if I had come home to find Shaman missing.

I think back to the question I asked our preacher back when I was ten years old with Paint safe in her stall. *Do animals go to heaven?*

When he uttered that loud "No," I realize now that he was answering with a logic based on his own very narrow version of religion. But there is something in me that goes back much further and disagrees strongly. In my heart I believe that people and horses and other animals have an older connection with an interrelated world that nourishes us. There is a mystery in this.

Do animals go to heaven?
I think I'll wait and see.

Online Glossary

For those of you who want more information about terms used in these stories and many others, go to WIKIPEDIA and play around.

Search for the GLOSSARY OF EQUESTRIAN TERMS and then look up:

Dressage
Horse Breeds
Warmblood
Arabian Horse
Hanoverian Horse
Thoroughbred
Quarter Horse
Lipizzaner
Dutch Warmblood
Airs Above the Ground
Piaffe
Leg Yield
Half Pass
Levade

About the Author

Letitia Sanders was born and grew up in a small town in Georgia where her pets were among her best friends. She followed her intellectual side to study English and creative writing and became Phi Beta Kappa at Sweet Briar College and Emory University.

After the death of her fiancé in Vietnam in 1967, she moved to San Francisco where she began a 24-year career working with computers for IBM. She progressed from programmer on the huge TOPS project, the largest real-time computer system in the world at the time, to becoming an instructor for IBM, traveling around the US, introducing new computers like the PC to IBM personnel and IBM customers.

She married Donn Downing, a retired *Time* magazine reporter who had reported from Vietnam and the White House. On weekends she rode Arabian horses in the coastal hills with a friend from whom she bought an Arabian colt named Shaman.

Upon retirement from IBM, Letitia completely deserted the computer world to work part-time at the ranch where Shaman was stabled. Her life became centered around horses, and she became a charter member of the California Nevada Arabian Sport Horse Association. Shaman's ability led her to join the US Dressage Foundation.

More recently, Letitia decided to exercise the writing talents she had studied in college. In a sense, she found herself back where she started, surrounded by animals and their stories.

Dear Reader:

I hope you enjoyed reading these stories about my years at the Ranch. I could not resist writing about the people and animals I met there. Perhaps you can feel my overriding theme of respect and love for animals. The way they relate to and enlarge us humans is a beautiful thing to experience, even if only in print.

If you have enjoyed this book, I would especially appreciate it if you would write a few sentences on the *Horses and Other Voices* page on Amazon. You can easily find it by going to my author page at **https://amazon.com/author/letitiasanders.**

Warm regards,

Letitia Sanders

Letitia Sanders

21063550R00106

Made in the USA
San Bernardino, CA
04 May 2015